MARIE TAYLOR-FORD

Hungry Hearts
at
Lilac Bay

LILAC BAY
SERIES
BOOK 1

For Mama
You will always be my inspiration

CHAPTER ONE

Brisk trade kept Lyra busy as she and her brother Silas manned The Pie-ganic, their food truck parked on the waterfront promenade of Lilac Bay. As Lyra slipped a cottage pie into a paper bag for a waiting customer, her eye was drawn to a movement along the water's edge. A toddler was wobbling around, getting precariously close to the unguarded bank.

"That kid's going to fall in," she said, shoving the bag at Silas. Without even pausing to take off her apron, she sprang down the two wire steps at the back of the truck and started running towards the child. Just as the little girl bent forward to peer into the water and almost toppled, a man dashed from nowhere to scoop her up. Lyra reached them, panicked and out of breath, as the man straightened up, clutching the child to his chest.

"You should keep a closer eye on your kid," Lyra said, irritated.

He was taller than Lyra and looked down at her with a frown, rubbing his free hand nervously through his short, thick hair.

"She's not mine."

The girl squirmed in his arms and he struggled to keep hold of her. Lyra's heart stuttered as they locked eyes, and she noticed his were the exact colour of the bay on an overcast day.

"If you're not careful, someone's going to think you're trying to kidnap her." Lyra's annoyance was turning to amusement. The man grinned.

A flustered-looking elderly man with several helium balloons tied to his wrist caught sight of them and waved. Lyra assumed he'd become separated from the child inside the nearby amusement park.

"Lucinda!" he yelled, and the little girl screeched and tried to twist herself free of the man holding her. He gently set her down and she toddled quickly towards the old man, who stooped to wrap her in a huge hug. He gripped her hand firmly as he made his way towards the waterside.

"Thank you." He arrived slightly out of breath. "She's too quick for my old bones."

"No problem," the man beside Lyra said, smiling. "She's definitely a fighter!"

"She is. I'm Reg and this, as you probably heard, is my granddaughter Lucinda." He extended his free hand.

"Alex." They shook hands. "Nice to meet you, Reg and Lucinda." He turned to Lyra. "This young lady here just about beat me to the rescue."

She felt her cheeks redden. "I'm Lyra," she said, avoiding eye contact and waggling her fingers at Lucinda, who was peeping from behind her grandfather's leg. "And I'd better get back to the truck before my brother has a riot on his hands." She gestured to Silas, who was dealing with a growing line of customers.

"Nice to meet you, Lyra," Alex called out after her. She shot a quick smile over her shoulder.

"Great work," Silas said, as Lyra washed her hands. "Now I need three liver pies, two steak and kidney, a cup of mashed peas…"

Lyra nodded and started humming as she helped Silas get the line of customers under control.

Alex stood talking to Reg and Lucinda a while longer, occasionally turning to look at Lyra. Each time, she quickly looked away. Peeking in their direction again, she spotted a middle-aged tourist wearing an American flag hat approaching the truck, frowning at the chalkboard menu as he drew closer. Lyra elbowed her brother.

"Oh, here we go," Silas said under his breath. "It's your turn, by the way."

She grinned. Silas hated explaining that "pies" weren't sweet in Australia, but Lyra thought it was a great ice-breaker. She'd had many interesting conversations with tourists after sharing that fact.

"Savoury pastry, meat fillings." She recited the spiel she knew well and truly by heart. "It's all part of the Aussie experience. And *this* is tomato sauce," she added, holding up a ketchup packet.

Curious, the man ordered a plain meat pie, smeared it with ketchup and took a huge bite right there in front of the truck.

"It's not *terrible*." He frowned as he chewed. He took another bite, dipping his head from side to side in deliberation. "Almost like a pot pie. I probably won't miss it, but I might be back while I'm still in Sydney."

"That's good enough for me," Lyra said, smiling.

She looked up at the shoreline. Alex, Reg and Lucinda were gone.

❖

The Pie-ganic was perfectly positioned beside the Lilac Bay ferry wharf, catching the morning commuter rush. That day, the rush went longer than usual and by the time it was over, the sun was high in the sky. The light glinted off the bobbing white boats moored along the bay's jetty and lit up the sandstone mansions beyond the ancient, twisted evergreens ringing the small inlet.

Lyra fixed herself a latte in the thermos she always brought, and stepped out to stretch her legs.

"I'll be back in fifteen. Just need to clear my head." Silas nodded, busy taking an inventory of pies and making notes in the ledger book he kept magnetised to the drinks fridge.

The bay was horseshoe-shaped and their truck was parked at the top of the semi-circle, close to the Sydney Harbour Bridge. Lyra wanted to avoid the late-season tourists, amusement park visitors and ferry passengers, so she headed in the opposite direction, towards the scoop of the bay. There was a small grassy area there, overlooking the quaint little white sand beach. Her favourite wood and stone bench was set in among the lilac bushes, and offered a view out through the mouth of the bay and into Sydney Harbour beyond.

She walked slowly along the dirt path in that direction, breathing the fresh salty air deep into her lungs, closing her eyes to feel the sun's warmth on her face. Every single day, Lyra and Silas felt as though they'd won the lottery with this view. Only two trucks had secured permits to sell along the Lilac Bay promenade boardwalk, but it had been several months since they'd claimed their spot and the second truck had yet to appear. They weren't exactly sure why; red tape was the best guess. That suited them perfectly, so they hadn't asked questions.

Lyra's bench was free when she reached it, and she sat down to enjoy the view. Autumn had always been her favourite season and today was a perfect example of why. The sun shone down, but the air had a crisp edge to it, and the punishing heat of summer was beginning to feel like a distant memory. It was quiet, and the only sounds that reached her aside from the waves lapping gently were the occasional jet-boat zipping past the bay entrance, distant screams from the amusement park roller-coaster, and the gentle dip of oars as a mother and son rowed out to their yacht.

She sipped her latte, toyed with the gold locket she always wore and leafed through her leather-bound notebook. She was still working on the same song she'd started a month ago. It had been happening more and more - Lyra would begin a song, but couldn't finish it. Or she'd go through periods with no new ideas at all. She kept telling herself it was just a dry spell, the kind every artist went through, and that eventually she would find the right notes. But she was anxious about it.

In any case, it didn't really matter. It had been ages since she and Mick, her keyboard player, had secured a real gig. She vowed to try and get one soon…maybe this week.

Lyra decided to try a new song in the meantime, and found herself writing a few lines about "the grey eyes of the bay." Absorbed, she didn't notice the time passing and was surprised when her phone rang. It was Silas.

"You've been gone forty-five minutes," he said grumpily. "I can see you, and I need to pee. Come back, please."

Lyra hung up the call and looked down at her notebook. Had she really just written part of a song about Alex? A random stranger she'd never see again? Embarrassed, she scratched her pen over the words she'd written. She tore out the page, crumpled it and tossed it in the bin, jogging back to the truck to give Silas a break.

CHAPTER TWO

"Sorry I'm late. Public transport nightmare," Lyra said to her two best friends as she slid into the third barstool around one of the oak barrels that served for tables at their local bar.

The Whistle Stop was a bit of a dive, but then that was its charm. The space itself was large and low-ceilinged, windowless but somehow always draughty. The floor was perpetually sticky and the decor was a mish-mash of kitsch. Vinyl booths lined the wall near the entrance, and the rest of the space was filled haphazardly with barrels and stools.

Amy and Marley had already ordered Lyra's usual vodka soda lime, the glass tantalisingly beaded with condensation. She blew them kisses and took a long, refreshing sip. "But I'll make up for it with a story about how I almost saved a life this morning."

"*Almost* saved a life?" Amy arched a perfect eyebrow. "Did the person die, or just not need saving in the end?"

Lyra grinned and took a moment to admire the beautiful new vintage dress Amy was wearing. It looked expensive, but that was nothing unusual - Amy was always flawlessly turned out, with her olden-day pinup curves showcased to perfection in retro-style clothes Lyra rarely saw her wear twice. She also had the face of an actual angel and was never without makeup or carefully styled hair. Tonight, Amy looked particularly exquisite, from the top of her blonde victory rolls to the tips of her red kitten heels.

Lyra was a jeans and t-shirt, ponytail, no makeup kind of girl. She always marvelled that Amy found that kind of time and energy to invest in her appearance, even on a weeknight.

Marley, on the other hand, usually seemed to have dressed inside a charity shop bin, in the dark. She was currently wearing a pair of blue-grey jodhpurs, teamed with a lime green top straight out of the eighties. Marley had delicate features and incredible bone structure, but she never did herself any favours with her dress sense. Silas often snidely referred to her as "Home Haircut".

As Lyra had filled Amy and Marley in on the morning's events with the little girl, leaving Alex out of the story for reasons she didn't really understand, they watched a beautiful blonde woman struggling to set up a guitar and mic on the little stage in the corner of the pub. She looked around helplessly, and was soon surrounded by a knot of men eager to help.

"They must be doing live music again here," Marley said. "You should try and get a gig, Lyra."

"I was actually thinking about that today. It's been a while. But I have no idea how it works here."

"Let's find out," Amy said, flagging down the next server that walked past. There was high turnover among the staff at the Whistle Stop, and Lyra had never seen this particular guy working there before. He had the kind of carefully scruffy look Lyra was often attracted to, with dark blond bed-hair and a smile that showed perfect teeth. As he approached their barrel, Lyra caught his unusual scent. A mix of cologne and strawberry shisha smoke.

"What can I get you beautiful ladies?" he asked, looking at each of them in turn. His gaze lingered on Lyra.

"You're new here?" Amy asked. "What's your name?"

"Miles." He gave her a big smile, leaning in closer. "Yeah, this is my second week. Nice of you to notice." His voice so close to Lyra's ear sent a thrill through her body.

"So, we have a question. Lyra here is an incredible singer." Amy gestured to Lyra, who flushed.

"Oh yeah?"

"Yes. How do you book gigs in this place?" Amy asked.

"Actually, I've started doing the bookings here now. It was kind of my idea to bring live music back. I'd be more than happy to work with you, Lyra." She smiled at him. "Just have your manager call me." He fished into his back pocket and held out a business card. After a split second of hesitation, and with a sinking heart, Lyra took it.

"Manager," Amy repeated flatly.

"Yeah, we only work with musos who have managers. Saves us a lot of time and that way we know they're professionals." Miles turned his gaze to the woman on stage.

"Great." Lyra swallowed hard and put Miles' card into her handbag. "I'll have mine call you."

Marley opened her mouth to speak, but stopped when Amy looped a leg around the barrel to kick her with a perfectly pointed heel.

"Thanks for the info, Miles," Amy said. "See you around." He touched Lyra's shoulder, giving her a long look, and then left. "I think he likes you," Amy said in a singsong voice to Lyra.

"The kiss of death!" Marley laughed, as Lyra put her head in her hands and groaned. It was an old joke between them. Lyra was totally fine around men, until she thought they were interested in her. Then she clammed up like a shell and more or less never recovered. "Oh, and why did you kick me, Amy?"

"You were about to tell Miles that Lyra doesn't have a manager."

"And?"

"And you don't always need to blurt out everything that comes into your head."

Several drinks later, the singer was halfway through her set and Amy was frowning. The woman's voice was off-pitch and her lyrics made little sense. She could also barely play three chords on her guitar and she couldn't play and sing simultaneously. Lyra found her very difficult to listen to.

"Oh God. She's terrible!" Amy plugged her ears dramatically. "I thought he said he works with professionals."

"Yeah, she's…." Lyra trailed off, blowing out a breath.

Amy held up a finger, then burped beautifully which made Marley collapse into giggles. "I have an idea. Lyra, you should *pretend* to have a manager." She slapped the table, sloshing a little out of their glasses.

"Ha-ha."

"No wait, hear me out, I'm serious. Bambi over there has the same amount of talent as my left ovary."

"Wait, didn't that get removed?" Marley asked.

"Exactly! But somehow, she's standing on this stage and you're not. Lyra, you're *actually* talented. So what if you don't have a manager? That shouldn't be the basis for anything. I say, you tell people you have a manager, and just pretend to be her as well!"

Lyra was silent a moment as she let Amy's words sink in.

"How would that even work?" Marley asked, twirling the

stick that skewered the lemon slice in her third glass of squash. Marley almost never drank alcohol.

"I don't know yet." Amy sipped her whiskey. Lyra had noticed that Amy was making eyes at a tall, shy-looking guy in the corner of the bar. Knowing Amy, she'd end up with this guy "walking her home." And soon. Lyra needed to hear the rest of the idea before Amy left. But her drunken brain seemed to be concentrating only on insignificant details.

"What would she be called? My fake manager."

"Oh. What about...Margot the manager," Marley said.

"Actually, that's not too bad." Amy nodded. "I like it. Margot sounds classy."

"What phone number would she have? Do I need to get a whole new phone contract?"

Amy shook her head. "Just don't say who you are. They ask for Margot, you're Margot. They want Lyra, it's you."

"I don't even know what a manager really does! Except that everyone always needs to speak to mine."

"They make phone calls with people like Miles and get you gigs!" Amy said. "And they take a cut of the money, I guess. In this case, let's just say Margot's rates are very competitive."

They laughed and Lyra noticed Shy Boy starting to work up the courage to approach Amy.

"What else do I need to know?" she asked.

"You'll need to add Margot's details to your posters and website, obviously." Amy positioned herself to showcase the best aspect of her ample bosom. "I can help with that."

"What else?"

"Oh for Pete's sake, Lyra. Figure it out yourself!" She grinned and winked at Lyra as Shy Boy finally approached the table.

"Uh, excuse me," Marley said sharply when he reached them, "we're trying to have a conversation here."

It was Lyra's turn to kick her under the table.

❖

After Amy left with her suitor, Marley and Lyra lasted another half hour before deciding to call it a night. Marley took a last minute bathroom break before her bus ride home, and while she was gone, Miles appeared beside Lyra. He cleared away their glasses and ran a wet rag over the barrel surface.

Lyra watched him, unable to think of a single witty thing to say. She smiled nervously when he caught her eye, noticing for the first time that there was a smattering of freckles across his nose.

"Lyra is a beautiful name, by the way." Lyra opened and closed her mouth, but nothing came out. She mentally rolled her eyes at herself. *The kiss of death.* "Give me your number," he added, sounding as calm as though he was talking about the weather, "could be fun to hang out sometime." He winked at her and held out his unlocked phone, open to the contact section.

With a thudding heart, Lyra tapped in her details. She still hadn't said a word and it occurred to her that if Miles had her number, she'd never be able to call him as "Margot". She made a mental note to ask Amy how to solve that riddle, as she handed the phone back to Miles. Before she could get her tongue untied, Miles tucked his phone back into his pocket, flashed her a quick smile and disappeared.

Lyra looked in the direction of the bathrooms for Marley, and found a mousy-looking barmaid staring back at her with narrowed eyes.

CHAPTER THREE

The next day was overcast and a storm appeared to be brewing on the horizon. As a result, there hadn't been a lot of foot-traffic coming through Lilac Bay. Lyra and Silas had more than enough stock left to keep The Pie-ganic open until after five, when people headed to the wharf to catch the ferry home.

"Got somewhere you need to be?" Silas asked Lyra, raising an eyebrow as he saw her check her watch and phone for the thousandth time. Silas was making notes in his ledger again.

Lyra tried to hide a smile. "I think I might have met some-one. I'm hoping to go see him again tonight."

She wondered how Silas would react. They didn't usually talk very much about things like this, Silas wasn't exactly a huge fan of conversations about their love lives.

Silas nodded. "Okay?"

"His name is Miles and he works at the Whistle Stop."

"Nice."

They stood in silence for a moment.

"You literally have no idea what to say to me, do you?" Lyra asked, grinning.

"You like a guy!" He shrugged. "I like them all the time. Are you two together then? Are you bringing him home? Have you slept together?"

"Oh good lord, Silas, *no!*"

"Ugh, you're such a prude!"

"I'm not a prude, I just like to take things a little slowly, that's all!"

The truth was that Miles hadn't texted her, and she didn't have his number to kick things off herself. And if she was perfectly honest with herself, she wouldn't have sent a message even if she did. There was no rush.

"Hey, look at that." Silas gestured past her.

"Ha-ha, Silas. If you don't want to talk about it-"

"No, really. Look at that."

Lyra turned in the direction he was pointing. A truck was carefully navigating along the thin strip of the promenade towards them. They exchanged a look...not this again.

A year earlier, they'd found a great spot right in the centre of downtown Sydney, in the business district. There were a few other trucks on the same block, and it had proved a popular and lucrative location for them - capturing the morning rush, office workers on their lunch breaks, the crowds as they headed home for their evening commute, as well as tonnes of foot traffic. There was a nice atmosphere of camaraderie among the food truck owners, and they'd often grabbed drinks together on a Friday evening.

Then one of the trucks on the block had changed owners. The new crew had started off by trying to make them all uncomfortable. There'd be a vaguely threatening note taped to The Pie-ganic overnight, or the shutter would be jemmied, or stock would go missing, or there'd be spray paint on their menu board. The siblings had spoken to some of the other food trucks on the block, who reported having the same issues.

As a group, they'd all gone to speak to the new vendor. No one could prove it was them, but the trouble had started when they had. In a very civil way, the group asked them to back off.

After that, things got much worse. One truck had its tyres slashed, the threatening notes became more explicit and eventually, one of the other trucks was even set on fire. No one had been injured, and the fire brigade had doused the blaze before it spread through the city. But the truck was a write-off and the owners had to go through a long battle with their insurance company to recoup not only the truck costs but the loss of income.

No one could prove it was anything but an unfortunate accident or mindless vandals, since the CCTVs in the area had been conveniently knocked out that night. To Lyra and Silas, that indicated a level of sophistication above and beyond petty criminals, and hinted at something bigger and more organised. They fled the scene.

Lyra saw Silas's jaw clench now. They had no solo claim to Lilac Bay and had always known in theory that another van would come. But it was one thing to know it and another thing to have it happen.

The afternoon sun bounced off the green panelling and Lyra couldn't make out the name, but just the sight of it was enough to make her heart feel heavier.

"Well, we aren't leaving now." Silas' eyes were fixed on the vehicle. "Oh, no," he said, catching sight of the van's name.

"*Meat is Murder?*" They read it in unison with the same tone of distaste. Lyra turned to Silas.

"Someone *actually* named their van that."

"No need to guess what their angle is," he said flatly.

"No. Or how they can guilt our customers into eating their food."

Silas chewed his lip as they stared at each other in silence, both wondering what this new truck would bring.

❖

Twenty minutes later, "Meat is Murder" was parked beside The Pie-ganic with its engine off, but the owner was yet to emerge.

"It's probably a hippy with musty hair who smells like patchouli."

"Leave patchouli out of this." Lyra laughed tonelessly. "Besides, maybe someone like that might actually be good for us. That's not everyone's cup of tea."

"All my meat is pastured and organic anyway," Silas said. "Says so right on our truck."

The sun had turned so that it was beaming directly into their van and despite the crispness of the day, Lyra was beginning to feel a little warm by the time Frank, one of their regulars, came out from the building where he worked in maintenance.

Lyra liked Frank. Originally from Italy, he had a relaxed and easy-going attitude and was always ready with an innocently flirtatious comment and a wink for either of them. As he walked towards them for his late afternoon pie fix - Lyra knew he'd have the chicken and vegetable, lots of tomato sauce, hold the mashed potatoes - he jerked his head in the direction of the rival van.

"Got some competition, I see," he said, gazing up at them.

Silas stuck his chin out. "We're not worried." He broke into a smile as he looked at Lyra. "She's our secret weapon. We might get her to do a little song for everyone who buys a pie."

Frank turned to her, pretending to be heartbroken. "Bella." He clutched his chest dramatically. "Six months I'm begging you to sing for me. If I knew this was all it takes, I would have called all the food trucks in Sydney to come!"

Lyra grinned at him, anxiety making her feel a little wired and cheeky.

"I'll do it. What's your request?"

Frank's eyes widened as he thought for a second, before coming out with the most unexpected answer: "Pink. Sober."

As Silas prepared Frank's pie, Lyra obliged and sang the song's chorus, pouring her heart and soul into it and forgetting for just a second that she was standing in a pie truck on a random Tuesday. It was the same energy she felt whenever she was on stage with Mick - something she could only describe as *transported.* When Lyra sang, it felt like she was doing what she was put on earth to do.

She opened her eyes to find Frank gazing at her with exaggerated rapture, while Silas's grin spread from ear to ear. And staring at her from a little distance away, silhouetted with the sun behind his back, was the owner of Meat is Murder, who had emerged from the truck.

CHAPTER FOUR

Lyra and Silas waited until Frank had gone, before they left the truck and approached the newcomer. He was busy setting up a sandwich board, and had his back to them. From behind, he seemed to be in rather good shape. Silas was a bundle of barely contained energy as they neared.

"Meat is *murder*?" Silas said to the man's back. "You do realise we're a pie stand? And that we sell *meat*?"

The guy froze and straightened up. He turned to them and Lyra's mouth dropped open in surprise.

"Alex?"

"Lyra?"

"What?" Silas said, confused.

"Uh, Silas, this is the guy that rescued that little girl last week, the one that almost fell in the water. Alex, this is my brother, Silas."

Alex was smiling at Lyra, and she felt her heart rate quicken, willing it to stop.

"You have quite a voice," he said. Lyra noticed that Silas shivered a little as Alex spoke.

"And you have quite a cheek with the name of your truck." Lyra was unable to keep a note of panic from her voice. "Are you allowed to be here? There are only two permits for this area and we heard the other one was stuck in some sort of legal confusion."

"Was stuck," Alex said, his eyes holding hers. "Is now unstuck."

Silas turned to Lyra, looking a little swoony. As passionate as he was about their food truck, she realised it was going to be a struggle for him to fight back if he was so attracted to Alex. She'd have to handle things for the two of them.

"Silas, I think there's a customer at the truck," she said, although there was blatantly no one around.

Alex stretched out his hand to shake Silas's in farewell. Silas shot Lyra a sidelong glance before he took it. He held it just a fraction too long and then Lyra was relieved when he headed back to the truck.

"So, you were here the other day to check out the competition then," Lyra said.

Alex held her gaze with his grey eyes, and she began to feel a little warm despite the chill of the day.

"It wasn't really like that," he said finally. "But I did want to see where I'd be working. Turns out, I think I'll enjoy the view…" He smiled, and Lyra's heart thudded in response.

"Yes, Lilac Bay is something else," she said, deliberately ignoring any innuendo. Then her eyes caught his sandwich board.

She and Silas used their sandwich boards to display their menu. Sometimes they switched it up and drew chalk pictures of their pies, or added a cute hand-written note to bring a smile to someone's face. Occasionally, they used the promotional sandwich boards their drink supplier gave them for free.

Alex's sandwich board showed vivid pictures of livestock being led to the slaughter.

"Is that some kind of joke?" Lyra asked, feeling real heat wash over her. She didn't think she had the strength to go through another battle like the one in the city.

Alex glanced back at his sign and then shrugged at her. "All's fair in love and war. Isn't that what they say?" There was an edge of sadness to his voice when he said it.

"I don't see why it has to be that way. You can just wait and see if anyone comes to eat your alfalfa salads and braised tofu."

"Those aren't on the menu but thanks for the suggestions." He smiled. "I'll try to play fair," he added, realising she was serious about an answer.

"Good. So you'll take that down."

"No, that has to stay. I won't be here long today, anyway. Supplier issues. Don't have a lot of stock. But I'll play fair aside from the sign."

Lyra sighed. "You can't guilt people into changing how they eat. That's why those horrible smoking ads don't work."

He shrugged. "We'll see, I guess."

Lyra turned to the water and took a few deep breaths, trying to calm her temper and her heart. Alex fiddled with the sandwich board, but didn't move to leave.

Lyra's phone rang, and she pulled it from her back pocket. It was the local hospital, so she knew it was something to do with Mick. He'd been experiencing a horrible streak of luck recently.

Alex was still standing beside her, so she pointedly turned away from him and slowly walked towards Silas, who was peering out of the truck at Alex.

"Lyra?" A familiar voice asked when she swiped to answer the call.

"Hey, Alison. What happened this time?" She was getting

to know Alison, a nurse in the emergency ward, quite well. They'd seen one another at the Whistle Stop once or twice by coincidence, but more often at the hospital - courtesy of Mick.

"Uh...you're not actually going to believe this." There was a note of awe in Alison's voice.

"It's Mick?"

"Yes..."

"Then try me."

She paused. "Lyra, it looks as though Mick's been struck by lightning."

❖

Lyra rushed straight to the hospital, after Silas agreed to run The Pie-ganic without her for an hour or two.

She found Alison still in the ward, changing the bag on Mick's IV drip as he slept.

"Is he okay?" Lyra was slightly out of breath from running straight out of the taxi and into Mick's ward, which was in an older part of the hospital she hadn't visited before. A single window looked out over the empty field behind the building and an old Venetian blind hung slightly askew over it, rattling gently in the air conditioner breeze.

Alison nodded, her red curls bouncing and her almond-shaped green eyes gazing at Mick in wonder.

"He's had some pretty strong painkillers and he's having a bit of a rest now. I put him back here so he could have a ward to himself. You'll have to tell him to buy a lottery ticket when he comes around. Some bush-walkers found him uncon-scious at the top of the bluff and called an ambulance."

Alison drew down Mick's bed sheet and showed Lyra his arm, where a livid red wound branched off over and over again like an actual lightning streak. Lyra let out a low whistle.

"It's kind of cool." Alison tucked Mick's arm back in. "At his age, it could have killed him. Listen, I have to move on. It was great to see you. In the nicest possible way, I hope it's a while before I see you again."

"I hear you."

They hugged and Alison picked up her clipboard and squeaked out in her scrubs and crocs, leaving Lyra to take a seat in the orange pleather armchair beside Mick and wonder for the thousandth time when her poor band member's bad luck streak would finally end.

She sighed, picked up a grimy, ancient Nat Geo and settled in to read about barnacles.

Mick woke up about an hour later, smacking his lips together thirstily. He struggled to focus on Lyra as she picked up the cup of water from his side table and guided the paper straw to his chapped lips. He drank a little, before coughing and resting back onto the pillow.

"Thanks for coming, kiddo," he said hoarsely after a moment. "What was it this time?"

"Can you move your arms?"

He tried, gingerly. "Yeah."

"Check out the left."

He raised it slowly, his eyes widening. "Is that...a lightning strike?"

"Yep."

"Huh." Mick was silent a moment, then gave her a cheeky look. "Guess I'd better go buy a lottery ticket."

CHAPTER FIVE

W hen Lyra got back to Lilac Bay a few hours later, after clarifying several times that Mick didn't need anything else, Alex's truck was closed up and Silas was taking a cigarette break by the side of The Pie-ganic.

Lyra had asked him a million times not to. "It brings the tone down," she would always say, and he would always reply, "It's a pie truck, Lyra. The jig is up."

He raised an eyebrow at her as she stepped into the truck, but she didn't give him the pleasure of saying anything about the cigarette.

As she tied her apron back on and surveyed their stock, Silas stepped back inside, shaking his head.

"So let me get this straight. So far this year - and we're only like a quarter the way through - Mick's gotten divorced, broken his nose, had his foot run over by a taxi," Silas ticked off the incidents on his fingers as Lyra admired his perfect manicure. Her nails chipped in two minutes but somehow, he kept his immaculate, "and now he's been struck by lightning?"

She nodded. "Don't forget the reason for his divorce. Steak and kidney?" she added hopefully, scanning the pie warming racks for her favourite flavour.

"Oh right. Wife left him for brother." Silas ticked off another finger. "And no, none left. Eat a liver, it's good for you."

She screwed her nose up at him.

"So, does Mick have brain damage now?"

"Gosh no. Got him in the arm."

"So he's fine?"

"Basically. He'll be out in two days."

"Can he still be your keyboard player?"

"I think so. He seemed to have the use of his arm. And he's going to have a pretty wild scar. Maybe I'll write him a recovery song and call it *Struck from Above* or something." She quickly pulled out her notebook and jotted down the line. Maybe this would be the moment her creative juices started flowing again.

"You know, sis," Silas tried to sound casual, but his tone immediately got Lyra's back up. She knew where this was going. They'd had this conversation a million times. "If you want to get serious about your music, you need to start working with someone else. You have talent. You could really do something with it. Mick's only holding you back."

Lyra lowered her pen and shook her head firmly, turning to face Silas.

"How can you even say something like that?"

Silas looked down. "I just mean that you could really do something, Lyra. *Really.*"

"Mick has stuck by me, by *us*, through everything. You don't just ditch people when it's not convenient. Besides, we vibe well together and there are very few people I can say that about in this world."

Silas looked slightly abashed. Lyra knew he loved Mick as

much as she did, but sometimes it was as though Silas had bigger dreams for her than she did for herself. And he was more ruthless with them.

"It's not like I'm ever going to crack the big time, anyway," Lyra continued. "We can barely book gigs, for goodness sake."

She grabbed a cloth and started cleaning the counter-tops - anything to avoid eye contact with Silas. But she could picture exactly how sadly he was staring at her and she couldn't bear it.

Mick had gone to high school with Lyra and Silas's father - they'd even played briefly in a band together - and had been like an uncle to the siblings when they were growing up. Mick had never stopped playing keyboard, and he was the first one who had encouraged Lyra to sing.

He and their father eventually had a huge falling out, but it had never affected the relationship between the three of them. And a couple of years later, their father had kicked Silas out. Lyra had followed him and Mick had taken them in. He was more than just Lyra's bandmate. He was their family.

"Stop cleaning," Silas said gently, and threw her a packet of chips as consolation for the lack of steak and kidney pies.

"If Mick dies, I'll get someone new." Lyra opened the chip packet.

"That man isn't going to die," Silas said, with grudging respect.

"I know! That's what I said to Alison!" Lyra spat a few crumbs in her haste to respond. Silas watched her with a mixture of amusement and disgust. "So, what are we going to do about Alex?"

"Enjoy having someone cute around? He's exactly my type."

"I have a bad feeling that he's going to steal a lot of our business."

"Surely not, with a vegan truck."

"It's not just that. Do you know what he said?" she asked.

"What?"

"'All's fair in love and war.' This could be another *war*. And we have to win."

Silas nodded. "Well. What are we going to do?"

"We need to steal that stupid sandwich board he had out today, for a start," Lyra said.

"We're not turning into thieves. Think straight for a moment. Our regulars are loyal. They know how much care goes into our food, and they like it. They like *us*. Maybe we don't have to do anything at all."

Lyra shook her head. "We do. The Pie-ganic is all we have. Who knows if Alex is part of the very same gang that ran us out before?"

Thinking back on that time, she opened one of the steaming containers on the warmer and stirred the peas so frantically that Silas gently took the slotted spoon from her.

"He looks nice," she continued, "but what if he's also an arsonist? We need to be on our toes. Let's not get sucked in like we did last time. Okay? We are *not* to be friends, or anything else, with this guy. Good-looking though he might be."

Silas nodded, and then fell silent for a moment, thinking. "Maybe we really can offer that you sing a little song for everyone who gets a pie?"

"That's sweet. But people just want to get their food and get on with it. They don't want their waitress warbling in their ears, not to mention how long the line would get!"

"Okay. What about..." he thought for a moment, then seemed struck by inspiration. "We could get some little stand-up tables, so that people don't have to carry everything

25

back to their desks right away, or find a bench along the bay. They can enjoy the sunshine and the view?"

Lyra thought for a second. "That's actually a really good idea, and I don't know why we're not doing it already."

Silas nodded. "See? We got this."

He started whistling and re-organising the drinks fridge.

Lyra pretended to be just as light-hearted, but inside, she was in turmoil. She didn't want to lose what they had. Maybe she hadn't given Alex a fair chance, but he had shown so far that he had some low tactics to bring in business. And it wasn't as easy as just picking up and moving to another place. They knew all too well from their experience in the city, the competition was hot and places scarce. Silas had confidence in them...Lyra just hoped he was right.

CHAPTER SIX

That weekend, Lyra and Amy helped Marley move into her new flat.

It was in a small block on a quiet street in the Inner West. The neighbourhood didn't have a lot of charm or character - Lyra didn't spot any restaurants, bars or cafes on her way in - but it seemed pleasant enough. There was a little grocery store a few streets down, and most of the other buildings nearby were either squat apartment blocks, or tiny one-storeys with concrete instead of front lawns. Still, it was a huge step up from the hostel where Marley had been living when Lyra first met her, and the five-person flat-share she was escaping with this move.

Marley was full of nervous energy, hauling loads of boxes up to the second floor so quickly that Lyra was worried she'd put her back out.

Lyra and Amy stood by the removal truck, taking a much-needed break.

"So, what happened with Shy Boy?" Lyra asked, and Amy ducked her head. "Oh my God, are you *blushing*?"

Amy held her chin up, a smile spreading over her face. "I

am not blushing, and nothing has happened yet. Well, not *that*," she added. Then she waved her hand, her red beret slipping slightly from her blond curls. She shoved her hands firmly into the pockets of her tailored slacks. "Let's talk about something else, I'm not ready yet!"

"Okay, okay. But don't keep me in suspense too long." Amy nodded. "Ugh, my arms are already so sore." Lyra massaged her biceps. "Silas and I went shopping for tables the other day, to put outside The Pie-ganic. We had to make sure I could carry them easily. Because of course Silas could lift them even if they were made of lead."

"Tables outside are a great idea." Amy raised her eyebrows. "How come you guys didn't think of it before?"

Lyra shrugged. "We never really had any need to innovate, I guess."

"So, Silas is into this Alex guy, huh?"

Lyra avoided Amy's eyes and scanned inside the truck for something she could carry up the two flights of stairs without injury. "Uh-huh. I guess so."

"What do you think of him?"

"I mean, *yes* he's good-looking. But I'm worried he's secretly part of that same gang of brutes from the city. And besides, as far as romance goes, I already started a little thing with Miles."

"What thing?"

"A liking thing."

"You can't multitask?"

Lyra laughed. "That sounds like something Silas would say."

"Your brother is a smart man."

"Hey!" Marley looked down at them from her Juliet balcony and tapped her watch with her index finger.

Amy saluted her and they giggled once she'd gone back

inside. They each slid a box from the back of the truck and made their way into the stairwell.

"Oh, I almost forgot to ask," Lyra said, heading up the stairs behind Amy. "Miles has my number. What am I supposed to do about Margot now?"

Amy shrugged like it was no big deal. "You can call him as Margot from my phone or something. Let's cross that bridge when we come to it. Does that mean you're going to do it? Bring Margot to life?"

"I'm going to talk to Mick about the whole idea tomorrow."

"That's great! I'm sure he'll say yes. That man would do anything for you."

"He's the best."

"Better than your real dad," Amy said with a huff.

"Well, that isn't difficult."

Amy stopped on the stairs, resting her box on one leg to catch her breath. She shook her head. "My mum's a pain in the bum, but she speaks to me. I can't believe you never hear from him."

"I can." After a DUI charge, her father had been forced by the courts to attend Alcoholics Anonymous meetings. There he'd met and married a hyper-religious woman who'd encouraged him to disown Silas after he came out. The whole relationship was an old wound Lyra didn't like poking around in. "Let's keep going."

"Sorry." Amy's face fell. "That was a really dumb way to phrase it."

"It's fine!" Lyra winked. "Stop using me as an excuse to rest!"

Amy laughed, and they huffed up the rest of the staircase. Lyra knew they'd be aching tomorrow in places they didn't know they had.

"Where do these go?" Lyra asked, entering the flat. It was

complete chaos. Boxes were stacked haphazardly around the living room and scattered in small piles along the short corridor leading to the small bedroom and bathroom. Furniture was placed randomly through the living room and kitchen. Marley hadn't labelled any of the boxes.

"Umm, the bedroom?"

Lyra's carton wasn't fully sealed, so she laid it down and moved to lift a flap.

"What are you doing?" Marley asked, her voice a little sharp. Lyra looked at her in surprise.

"I just thought I'd see if it looked like bedroom stuff."

"Please don't do that."

Lyra and Amy discreetly shared a look. Lyra held her hands up. "Okay, sure. Sorry. I'll move it to the bedroom." She heaved it up, heading down the corridor.

The bedroom needed a thorough clean. The floor was caked with dust and the windows were almost frosty with grime. It had been a while since anyone had rented this place, by the looks of things.

There was a chest of drawers by the window and a new, plastic-wrapped mattress leaned up against the wall. Lyra stacked the box neatly beside the drawers, then as she was crossing back out of the room, the afternoon light glinted off something on the floor. She bent to pick up a gold necklace with a letter "L" charm dangling from it.

"Check this out," Lyra said to Marley back in the living room, where she was re-stacking some of the smaller boxes. Amy was gone, already on her way down to do another load. "Someone here before you must have lost it."

Marley held her hand out and examined the chain for a second. "It's junk, I'll throw it out."

Lyra nodded, but as she moved back into the stairwell for another trip to the truck, she caught a motion out of the corner of her eye. Marley had turned her back to Lyra, not realising she was still there. She slipped the chain into her pocket and held her hand in there for a long moment, seemingly lost in thought.

Lyra found it odd, but sometimes Marley herself could be odd.

"I need a break," Lyra said to Amy, back at the truck. "I'm going to have to see my chiropractor after this!"

"Come on," Amy groaned, ignoring Lyra as she wrestled with a large box. "We're going to be here all day if we don't hurry!"

Lyra stopped clutching her lower back and moved to help Amy. Marley had promised them dinner in return for helping her move. Right now, Lyra was ready to order the lobster. Preferably fed through the face hole of a massage table.

When the truck was finally unloaded, the girls sat on towels on Marley's gritty living room floor to eat fish and chips and share a bottle of red wine.

"I have no idea where the glasses are though." Marley glanced around.

"You didn't think to label the boxes?" Lyra couldn't help asking.

Marley shrugged. "I honestly didn't realise I had this much stuff."

"It does accumulate, doesn't it?" Amy unscrewed the wine cap. She raised her eyebrows at Lyra, who nodded, giving Amy permission to swig straight from the bottle. It would only be the two of them drinking, and there wasn't really another option.

"I moved to Sydney, what, two years ago?" Marley asked, and Amy nodded. The two of them had met at a painting class right after Marley had moved here. Amy had introduced Marley and Lyra several months later. "And all I had was a suitcase. One suitcase! Now look at this."

Lyra looked around. It was definitely a lot. Lyra wondered how on earth Marley was going to sort through it all, and how long it would be in this state. She was beginning to feel claustrophobic and itchy just looking at it all.

"What are your plans now that you're finally an independent woman without hideous flat-mates to worry about?"

"Ugh," Amy said, before Marley could answer. "I honestly don't know how you had flat-mates for almost two years. I would have jumped out the window."

"I didn't really have a choice." Marley popped a chip in her mouth. "I had to get my feet on the ground first. Now I have a proper job and my own place. I have big plans and I can finally get started with them."

Marley had taken a job as a receptionist with a local doctor. "How are you liking the job?" Lyra asked. "The general public can be pretty exhausting, in my opinion!"

"The doc's a little bit scatter-brained, and she keeps trying to get me to wear a uniform."

"Wouldn't it be nice not to have to think about what you're going to wear?" Amy asked, as tactfully as she could. Marley's eccentric sense of style probably wasn't a great fit for a doctor's office.

Marley shook her head vigorously. "No. I can't imagine anything worse."

"Fair enough," Lyra said. "It should be the work that counts and nothing else."

"I've installed a system for patient record keeping and appointment taking. She's been doing everything on paper, can you believe it?"

"What?" Lyra and Amy were shocked.

Marley nodded. "I know. It's going to take me ages to type

all the records in, but eventually we'll be able to go to online booking as well. At the moment, she's really limited to the number of patients she can take, because she's still hand-writing their medical notes."

"You're going to save her so much money and probably bring in a tonne of new business as well," Amy said, impressed.

"I hope she's paying you well."

"It's enough that I can easily afford the rent here," Marley said. "I know it's not the most beautiful place, but it will work well for me."

"I wish we could raise our glasses to you," Amy said, looking around. "But let's settle for clinking some chips together."

They each took a chip and held it aloft.

"Here's to totally reinventing ourselves," Marley said. Lyra found it a strange toast, but as someone about to possibly reinvent herself as a singer with a manager, she wasn't in a place to point fingers.

They tapped the chips together and toasted it.

CHAPTER SEVEN

Lyra paid Mick another visit in hospital the following day. He looked much better and was sitting upright in the hospital bed with his arms crossed and lightning wound on display. His face was grizzled with stubble. Lyra told him Amy's idea about Margot the manager.

"You're actually considering it?" Mick asked. The colour had returned to his face and his movements were more fluid. He'd been discharged already, and then re-admitted due to unusual heart rhythms which were being monitored. Alison thought he'd be back out again that day, and Lyra was excited to jam together once he was fully recovered.

"I think it can work, don't you?" She leaned forward in the visitor's chair. "What do we possibly have to lose? And it might get us more gigs."

Mick surveyed her, then shrugged. "Okay, kiddo. If you want to try, why the heck not?"

Lyra leapt up and kissed his stubbly cheek. He laughed.

"Trying to give me a heart attack?"

"Don't even joke about it! And when you leave this place, you are *taking* the wheelchair."

Once when Mick was being released from hospital, he'd been too proud to be wheeled off the ward. But he'd become dizzy while walking out, smacked his head on a door jamb and been instantly re-admitted to the neurological ward. This time Lyra wasn't going to let him take any chances.

Alison entered the room at that moment. "Tell him, Alison! Not leaving here unless it's on wheels."

She looked up and her eyes were puffy and bloodshot.

"Huh?" She stared at Mick's chart without comprehension.

Mick shot Lyra a concerned look. She stood up from the chair, the plastic velcroing off her skin with a sucking sound, and met Alison at the foot of the bed.

"Do you have time for a quick coffee, Alison?" she asked gently. "I'd love to talk about Mick's discharge papers."

She looked at Lyra, her eyes filling with tears.

"Come on," Lyra said, guiding her out of the room. She shot Mick a look over her shoulder and he frowned.

They walked down a corridor and Lyra led Alison into the emergency stairwell, where she thought they'd be less likely to run into nosy co-workers.

"I can't stay away long," Alison said and then began to sob, dropping her head into her hands.

Lyra patted her awkwardly on the back, not sure they knew one another well enough for the hug she felt tempted to give. Alison fished a tissue out of her pocket and blew her nose loudly.

"Sorry." Her face was blotchy and red. "My boyfriend...I guess ex-boyfriend, it's really over now. I've moved out. It's my fault. I cheated, and it hadn't been working for a while, but now it's real and-" she choked off, unable to finish the sentence.

"Oh, crap. Alison, that sucks." Lyra gave her a proper hug as Alison drew some bracing breaths. "How long were you two together?"

"Two years. I know it's silly to be this upset when I was the cause, but I can't help it."

"I'm so sorry. You deserve to be with someone you really love. Everyone deserves that."

Alison nodded, looking wretched. "The worst part is I'm going to have to live with friends for a while. It's embarrassing that we couldn't make it work." She started sobbing afresh.

"Hey, hey, listen to me," Lyra said, and Alison looked up, sniffing. "You've got nothing to be embarrassed about. People don't tend to cheat when they're happy with their partners. Yes, it's a shame it got to that stage, but you'll both recover."

"I guess you're right." She blew her nose again.

"Are you together with the guy you cheated with now?"

Alison screwed up her nose and shook her head. "He was just some idiot I met in a bar. He wasn't worth it at all." Her eyes welled up again.

"Well, never mind," Lyra said quickly. "It's definitely going to hurt badly for a while, but then it will hurt less and then suddenly there'll be a day where you just don't think about the situation at all. And that day's closer than you think." Lyra was doing her best to sound reassuring.

Alison nodded and wiped her eyes, managing a tight smile. "Thank you, Lyra. This really helps. Ugh." She blew her nose a final time and squared her shoulders. "I'd better get back to it before I lose any patients!"

Lyra nodded and went back to Mick's ward.

"She okay?"

"Breakup," Lyra answered, sitting down beside him.

"Poor kid."

"It was her fault."

Mick shook his head. "There's always two sides."

"Even when one person cheats?" Lyra asked, surprised. She knew Mick's wife had cheated on him and left him for his brother. But that was the kind of guy Mick was. Never bitter, never cruel, never looking back.

"Even when one person cheats," he said firmly. Lyra found it odd that he was so sure.

CHAPTER EIGHT

Lyra leaned on the counter of The Pie-ganc with her face in the sun, reading a paperback and waiting for the lunchtime rush to start while Silas unboxed cutlery. They'd set out the standing tables as planned and seen a corresponding bump in traffic and repeat purchases.

The weather was once again perfect for mid-Autumn. Mild and with a gentle breeze bringing the scent of lilac. A jet boat sped past and the occupants waved and whooped happily as some gulls wheeled overhead. Lyra thought for the millionth time how wonderful it was to be able to work on the waterfront.

She pulled her phone from her back pocket and opened it to the message Miles had sent at 11pm the night before. *What's up? ;)*. His first message, and Lyra had already been asleep when it arrived. As yet, she hadn't thought of anything witty to respond.

She snapped a pic of the beautiful waterfront before her, including just the top edge of her paperback in frame. *At work,* she texted, attaching the photo and adding a smiley emoji. Her finger hovered over the send button for far too long. She told herself she was over-thinking things, and finally sent the message off, shoving the phone back into her pocket.

"Maybe we scared him off?" Silas said, with just a top-note of disappointment in his voice. "It's halfway through the week and he hasn't come back."

"Alex? He was having supplier issues, maybe they got worse. We can only hope. Anyway, I'm sure he'll be back, he seems the annoying type." She turned a page in her book.

"You really think so?"

Lyra snapped the book shut and turned to her brother, giving him a look. "Silas. Repeat after me. This guy is our enemy. Or at least, we don't know yet that he *isn't*."

"Yes, yes. Enemy. Got it. How was Mick, anyway?"

"He's fine, or almost fine. Doing much better now he's at home. I hate seeing him in that hospital bed."

"Still can't believe it happened."

"I know. I genuinely can't tell if he's super lucky to have survived it all, or super unlucky that it all happened in the first place."

"I'll take option two for a hundred bucks."

"Why haven't you been to see him?" she asked. Silas suddenly busied himself inspecting a tiny fleck on the glass of the fridge. He shrugged.

"I've had a lot going on."

Lyra pushed herself up off the counter and looked at him. "You've been weird with Mick for a while now. It's almost as though you don't care. You remember he took us in when Dad kicked you out, right? How good he's always been?"

"Yes." Silas nodded. "Everything's fine. I'll visit once soon. Take him some pies."

They fell into silence for a while. Lyra served a young family. The little girl sat perched on her father's shoulders, a helium balloon tied to her wrist. They had obviously just come from the amusement park. It reminded Lyra of the first day she had met Alex. She pushed that thought out of her mind.

After the family left, a woman jogged up, pulling a Blue-tooth earphone out as she neared.

"Welcome to The Pie-ganic," Lyra said. "What can I get for you?"

She wrinkled her nose. "Ew, no meat thank you. I was wondering when that other truck was coming back?"

The smile froze on Lyra's face. "What other truck?"

"The one with the vegan options. It was right here a couple of days ago."

Lyra turned to Silas, who was looking grim. A flash of inspiration struck her and she turned back to the woman. "I know the one you mean. That truck was unfortunately suspended for hygiene reasons. The owner got slapped with quite a few health code violations."

"Really?"

Lyra nodded. "Cockroaches in the storage bins was the least of it. Can I offer you some vegetable chips as an alternative?" She showed her the packet. "Only one third the fat of potato chips."

The woman shrugged, bought them, plugged her ear back up and jogged off. Silas and Lyra high-fived...and moments later, spotted a green truck turning down the promenade.

❖

"Thought you were rid of me, I bet," Alex yelled towards them as he set up the offending sandwich board again. Just in time for the lunch rush.

"More like hoped!" Lyra called back, feeling apprehensive. Alex strolled over.

"Supplier issues." Lyra nudged Silas. "But I'm back, stronger than ever. I like the tables. That's a really good idea."

"So will we see the same thing outside your truck tomorrow?" Lyra said.

"She's funny, Silas, isn't she?" Alex tried to include Silas into the conversation, but he grabbed a cloth and made himself busy cleaning a non-existent mess.

"May the best truck win today," Lyra said.

"I didn't do so bad when I was here last time."

"Didn't do great either, though…" Lyra shrugged one shoulder at him. He grinned and she turned away.

The first customers out for lunch started to wander over. Frank was among them. Lyra and Silas thought they were safe with him, but he wandered over to Alex's truck and spoke to him for a few moments. Lyra couldn't help feeling betrayed, but Frank came over to them a moment later.

"His drinks are a dollar more each than yours," he reported. "And I don't understand half of what's on the menu."

"You just earned yourself a free drink with your pie," Lyra said.

"Ah, Bella. I would happily spy for you anytime!"

He gathered up his chicken pie and soft drink and stood at one of the tables in the sun.

The next two customers, a plump man and woman holding hands, headed over to Alex's truck. Silas and Lyra exchanged glances, but only the woman bought something from Alex. The man came over to them and bought a pie and two drinks, standing at their tables to eat.

Lyra saw one woman heading for The Pie-ganic until she caught sight of Alex's sandwich board. Tears sprang to her eyes. She hesitated between the two trucks and eventually went for his. Lyra saw her clutching plastic utensils when she left and filed that away as a selling point for them to promote - Silas had always insisted they use compostable cutlery.

The woman was in the minority though. Most people who saw Alex's sandwich board either made faces of disgust, or told the siblings they thought it was manipulative.

At some point, Lyra switched on the radio to help bring down her stress levels, and they discovered that even more of the crowd was drawn to them that way. They'd rarely had as much foot traffic, and there was always a small queue waiting to use the tables. Lyra was in a good mood seeing people trickle towards Alex but flow towards them.

For a couple of hours, she was really enjoying herself. At least until she checked her phone and saw that Miles had read the message but hadn't responded.

❖

When the rush had tapered off, Alex paid them a short visit.

"Nice work," he said. He genuinely didn't seem annoyed, which Lyra found odd. "Seems people don't care as much about animal cruelty as I thought."

"That's because they know we aren't responsible for any," Lyra said. "I'm telling you, that sign isn't a good idea for your business. Although I don't know why I'm helping you," she added, irritated with herself.

Alex smiled and there was an awkward silence as their eyes held for a beat too long. "What do you both usually do once you finish up here each day?" he asked, his tone light.

Silas lifted his head and looked between the two of them, a frown darkening his features. "She's spoken for."

"Silas, he's not asking me out! Just what we do after work." Silas shrugged and turned away. Lyra debated whether or not to correct what he'd said. She didn't like the idea of Alex thinking she was with someone, although she couldn't quite pinpoint why. "Have you seen Reg and Lucinda again?" she asked, smiling to try and take the bite out Silas's words.

"No." Alex gave her a tight smile in return. "I'll see you both tomorrow, have a great evening."

He headed back to his van, quickly packing up. He tooted his horn as the truck inched back down the promenade.

"I think he likes you," Silas said, heaving one of the tables towards the truck when they prepared to leave an hour or two later.

"Oh, great. Another kiss of death." Lyra sighed. "You didn't have to lie about me being in a relationship." She was unable to keep an edge out of her voice.

"What, do you like him too?" Silas asked, almost losing his grip on the table.

"No. I'm following my own advice not to get involved. Remember?"

"Oh, I remember. Do you?"

"I already told you I'm interested in someone else. Although you made it sound *a lot* further along than it is."

Lyra knew she should have been pleased that Silas had forced a wedge between her and Alex. They knew nothing about him, and where their business was concerned, he hadn't made the best first impression. She wasn't sure how much Silas still thought about the fights in the city, but she still thought about them often. Occasionally she had dreams she was trapped in a burning truck. There was no way she wanted to go through that kind of situation again.

CHAPTER NINE

Amy peered into her laptop, scanning Lyra's website which she had just updated. They were sitting at the marble-topped counter in Amy's living room, perched on green velvet stools beside one another.

"I think that looks good, don't you?"

Lyra nodded. It wasn't much of a website, more like a page with a couple of photos and some samples and videos embedded. It was Lyra's answer to the constant refrain of "get online", heard whenever people found out she was a singer. Everyone was on Instagram and Spotify or TikTok apparently and she couldn't imagine anything worse.

Until today, Lyra's website had also listed her as the contact for gigs and bookings. Thanks to Amy's handiwork, Margot the Manager was now listed front and centre. She had been born with a single sentence: All bookings and enquiries to Margot Hunter, Entertainment Manager.

"What if people think, 'I know everyone in the business and there's no Margot Hunter'," Lyra asked, concerned.

"Fake it till you make it, babe." Amy snapped her laptop shut.

"Amy...doesn't this make me a liar?" Lyra knew Amy's rules on lies were fairly unforgiving, so she was surprised Amy had not only suggested the idea of a fake manager, but was helping follow through on it.

Amy shook her head firmly. "This is correcting an imbalance in the universe. It's completely unfair that something as arbitrary as whether or not you're paying for a manager should be the deciding factor in what opportunities come your way. Besides, you only have to keep her until you get a real one. It's more like make believe. And now," she added, with a twinkle in her eye, "Margot is going to make her first call."

"Tonight?" Lyra's voice came out in a higher pitch than she intended.

Amy walked to her liquor cabinet and put a manicured finger on her lips as she scanned its contents. "Yep," she said firmly. "Tonight."

Amy's apartment always made Lyra feel like she was in the presence of a proper adult. It was small, but perfectly designed and exactly reflected Amy's character. The walls were painted in chic shades and hung with proper artwork and custom-made neon signs. The lighting was moody and flattering, different textures created warmth and cosiness, she had expensive rugs and a proper, grown-up sofa. Everything in her place was immaculately styled. A tour of her home had even been featured on *Apartment Therapy.*

Amy was the star of the small interior design firm where she worked. She always had more clients wanting to work with her than she could take on.

As Amy started mixing Moscow Mules, complete with oversized ice cubes, chilled copper mugs and glass straws, Lyra thought back to their last evening at the Whistle Stop.

"Oh, I can't believe I haven't asked again," she said, slapping her forehead. "What's the latest with Shy Boy?"

Amy grinned. "Seeing him again this weekend."

"No way! I have never known you to say that with a smile on your face."

"Sure you have." She chuckled.

"Usually I hear, 'he wants to see me again, I said yes but I'm going to flake'."

"I'm not that bad...am I?"

"You are and I love it. What's so special about this guy?"

Amy set the drinks down on the counter and joined Lyra on the other stool. She shrugged, looking almost coy.

"He's just really different. He's...argh! I don't know. Let's just wait and see, okay? I hate talking about this stuff, I feel like it jinxes it."

"I get it. Let's talk about Miles then."

"No," Amy said firmly. "Let's talk about Margot and the launch of your career with a manager."

She pulled a working, vintage rotary dial phone over to the counter. She was the only person Lyra knew who still had and legitimately used a landline.

"What's happening?" Lyra asked, taking a deep sip of her cocktail.

"Margot is making a booking. Or at least an inquiry."

"With who?"

"Let's not start out with Miles. We'll do a different place to get Margot into the swing of things and then we'll call him up another time."

Lyra sucked on her straw as Amy prised the cocktail from her grasp. She slid it behind her back.

"But I need it for courage."

"You'll get it back once Margot gets a booking."

"I wouldn't have a clue where to start! I don't know the numbers of places who even have live music off the top of my head."

"I know one," Amy said, sipping delicately and raising her eyebrows. "Dial this number."

Lyra tried to reach around Amy for one last sip of her cocktail, but she was too quick.

"Six five one," Amy began loudly, and Lyra had to scramble to catch the numbers. She took a deep breath as the phone started ringing. Confidence on stage was so much different to the kind of confidence it took to do this. "Ask for Rusty."

The phone was picked up by a polite-sounding older woman. There was a gentle buzz of conversation and laughter in the background, which Lyra took as a good sign.

"Hi, can I please speak to Rusty?"

"Sure, love. Who can I say is calling?"

"Tell him it's Margot Hunter."

"He know what it's about?"

"I was told to call him."

"Alright, love, hold on." The woman yelled for Rusty as Amy nodded encouragingly. Lyra reached for her drink but Amy blocked her hand, and pointed to the phone. Lyra heard crackling as the phone was passed over. An older-sounding man announced his presence with a simple: "Rusty."

"Hello, Rusty," Lyra took a deep breath and plunged in head first. A kind of calm came over her and she made her voice sound important and unhurried. "My name's Margot Hunter and I represent a singer named Lyra and her keyboardist Mick. I'd like to talk to you about booking them for your venue."

Ten minutes later, Lyra and Mick had a gig, and it's possible Rusty had a crush on Margot. Lyra thought *she* might have had a crush on Margot, she was so unflappable and confident. Amy gave her a round of applause and slid the drink back as Lyra hung up the phone.

"That was awesome!" She high-fived Lyra. "Margot crushed it."

"She did, didn't she?" Lyra was unable to keep a goofy grin off her face. "Amy, thank you for the idea and thank you for pushing me!"

They clinked copper mugs and, with that out of the way, they were free to relax, let the evening begin and drink as much as they liked.

❖

The night continued the way it often did with Lyra and Amy, both of them trying to outdo one another with ever-cheesier songs to which they danced badly.

"Should I ask Miles out?" Lyra asked, when they slumped onto the sofa for a dancing break. Miles hadn't replied to her text, but then "at work" didn't really warrant an answer. Lyra was annoyed at herself for not having asked a question, so he'd need to reply. Amy screwed up her nose. "What?"

"I just…" Amy sighed. "I'm not entirely sure he's good enough for you." She shrugged. "Sorry."

Lyra had met Amy in their late teens, in one of the many flatshares she and Silas had moved in and out of. They'd clicked immediately and had been in each other's lives ever since. Amy was the closest thing to a sister Lyra would ever have and it was important to her that Amy approved of the guy she liked.

"Of course he's good enough for me," Lyra scoffed, grabbing a cushion and hugging it to her chest. "You're being over-protective."

"I'm being exactly the right amount of protective." Amy softened. "I could totally change my mind if he proved himself worthy. I'm just yet to be convinced." Lyra raised an eyebrow and Amy threw her hands up. "Go ahead and ask him out then. I shall reserve my judgement." She zipped her fingers across her lips.

Lyra stared at her phone for a minute, trying to imagine putting herself out there enough to ask Miles out. She decided she'd already overcome enough challenges for one day.

"I'll do it another night!"

Amy nodded, then dragged Lyra up off the couch to continue the dance-off.

As she was leaving in the small hours, Lyra glanced at a family portrait in the hallway. Some puzzle pieces clicked into place in her drunken brain.

"Amy!" She spun to face her and thumped her arm harder than she intended to.

"What was that for?" Amy said, rubbing her arm and catching her balance - in her drunken state, the blow had nearly toppled her.

"I have seen this family portrait so many times. I know everyone in it."

A grin was spreading slowly across Amy's face. "And?" she said innocently.

"I especially know who that is," Lyra jabbed her finger onto the figure in the portrait, "even though I've never met him in real life."

"Do you?" Amy shrugged, but her smile was betraying her.

"Yes! That is your Uncle Russell, better known as Rusty. Owner of Rusty's Pub!"

Amy burst out laughing. "I knew you'd need a win on Margot's first call. But trust me, Uncle Russ isn't inviting you to sing as a favour to me. I played him some of your originals and he couldn't wait to have you and Mick gig there."

"You are so naughty." Lyra suddenly became emotional,

tears springing to her eyes. "Thank you." Lyra hugged Amy tightly and buried her head into her neck. "Thank you."

Amy hugged back just as tightly. "You're so welcome."

Lyra left wondering what on earth she'd ever do without girlfriends like hers.

CHAPTER TEN

Alex's truck had pulled up late and he was yet to emerge from it. Lyra was fairly certain that was why Silas was stretching out his cigarette break. Eventually he gave up and came inside, picking at his nail as Lyra ignored him and continued reading. A low warm breeze was ruffling the water and foot traffic was scant.

"Glad he took that sandwich board down," Silas said.

"He doesn't get props for that. Shouldn't have had it up in the first place." Lyra didn't look up from her book.

"Still. It's been a good few days for both trucks this week. I think it's all going to work out."

"Mmm."

A few moments later, Lyra heard a strange noise and glanced in Alex's direction. She slapped her book shut. "You're kidding me," she said, unsure whether to be amused or infuriated.

"What?" Silas was immediately on the alert. He leaned out of the truck and blinked several times before leaning back in and facing Lyra, biting his lip. "Maybe he's always had it?"

"He's always had a lamb with him and we've just never

noticed?" Lyra put her hand on her hip as Silas shrugged. "I'm going to have to fight this battle alone, I can see."

"What do you suggest we do?"

"I'm sure he doesn't have a permit for it...if you need permits for animals. Surely it's unhygienic? But with that there, do you really think anyone will eat a shepherd's pie today?"

"No. You're right."

Before Silas could stop her, Lyra took off her apron and headed to the small makeshift enclosure beside Alex's van. It was complete with AstroTurf flooring and a huge pile of fresh grass clippings. Alex was crouched beside the lamb, patting and whispering to it.

"You brought an apprentice, I see."

Alex turned around at the sound of her voice and smiled, straightening up. "Oh, hey Lyra. This is Murgatroyd. Murgatroyd, say hi." Murgatroyd and Lyra ignored each other. "Cute, isn't he?"

"Should I even ask why that's here?"

"He."

"He should surely be on a farm, frolicking in... frolicking with his mother?"

Alex shook his head, grey eyes twinkling. "Don't talk about mothers in front of Murgatroyd." He leaned towards her and she caught the scent of laundry soap. "He was rejected by his mother," he whispered in her ear.

Lyra didn't flinch, but she felt a thrill run down her spine at his closeness. Before she could reply, there was a loud squeal. They both turned to see Jogging Lady stepping over the pen wall to get close to Murgatroyd, who first skittered away from her, then tentatively drew closer.

"He is *adorable,"* she beamed up at Alex.

"I was trying to convince this young lady of the exact

same thing." He jerked his thumb towards Lyra. Jogging Lady looked up.

"Oh, I remember you," she said, standing. One hand lingered on Murgatroyd's soft head. "You're from that meat truck-"

"Pie."

"You told me his truck was closed down because of-"

"Anyway!" Lyra turned quickly. "I'd best be setting up for lunch."

"Wait just a second," Alex said, putting a hand out towards Lyra. "What exactly did she tell you about the truck?"

They both looked at Jogging Lady, who couldn't keep a smug look from her face. "That it was closed down for hygiene violations."

"I'm so sorry, you must be mistaken," Lyra said, wriggling out of Alex's grasp. "I would never have said such a thing. Although, with the lamb here…"

"I'm setting up a handwashing station. And we'll only be here a few hours a day."

Jogging Lady put a hand on her hip, shooting Lyra a *so there* look. Lyra walked quickly back to The Pie-ganic

"Cheat!" Alex called after her, and she waved over her shoulder, struggling to hide a grin. It seemed the kiss of death had never kicked in when she was around Alex, for some reason. Maybe it was because Lyra didn't truly believe he was interested in her.

Back in the truck, she started organising chip packets with so much energy that Silas grabbed her hands to stop her from crushing them. "We need to step up our game again," she said.

"How?"

"I don't know. You're the brains of this outfit."

"Since when?"

"Since you came up with the table thing. Access that place in your mind again, sir. We need it."

"Well, I don't know how to compete with a lamb." He shrugged.

Lyra scratched her head, watching as people started flowing along the promenade and heading towards Murgatroyd for a pat. It looked as though Alex's ploy was going to work, or at least get people's attention no matter which truck they chose for their food.

"I've got it!" she said.

"Spill."

"A vegetable pie."

Silas was silent and she could see the wheels turning.

"Actually," he said finally, "I do have a really good recipe for a vegetable pie filling. I guess I could try it out."

"Perfect." She turned to welcome some customers.

Silas spent the next hour jotting little notes down and looking more and more pleased with himself.

"I think the veggie pie might be the best one yet! I'll head over to Jan's tonight and get a few made up."

Lyra and Silas had searched exhaustively for a supplier they felt comfortable with before starting The Pie-ganic. As soon as they'd met Jan, they knew the search was over. A powerhouse of an older woman, purple-haired Jan and her small team worked directly with local farmers for their meat and produce, made small batches of wares in their commercial kitchen and followed Silas's recipes to the letter. Jan only worked with a handful of clients and they'd never been let down in quality or reliability.

Lyra slapped Silas on the shoulder. "That's wonderful. Now please hurry up with the mashed potatoes."

Later in the afternoon, towards the end of the lunchtime rush, a gang of teenage boys wandered past. Dressed in hooded sweatshirts and running shoes far more expensive than it looked like they could afford, they smoked cigarettes and tossed the butts, along with the cans of beer they sipped, right into the bay.

They stopped for a while, staring at both the food trucks, and Lyra heard them scoffing at Silas for "wearing makeup". Silas sometimes lined his eyes with black kohl, which Lyra thought made him look even more beautiful, if such a thing were possible.

The teenagers pointed at Murgatroyd and doubled over with laughter. One of them started making sudden, loud shrieking noises, and Murgatroyd began skittering around his pen in obvious distress.

A member of the group, slightly shorter and thinner than the others, looked upset at the turn of events involving Murgatroyd. He tried to stop his friend from shrieking, but instead the whole group turned on him. He held up his hands and took a few steps back. The shrieking resumed.

Lyra had been waiting for them to leave so she could fish their garbage out of the water before it was carried off. But when she saw Murgatroyd upset, she couldn't stay still any longer.

"Where are you going?" Silas asked as she took off her apron.

"That poor lamb is freaked out."

"I thought you hated it? They're just dumb teens posturing. They're not going to do anything and they'll be gone in a second."

"What is the matter with you lately?" she asked. "Why are you so detached from everything?"

Silas bit the side of his mouth and looked down. "Sorry. Want me to go check the lamb?"

She shook her head. "No, you'll disappear inside Alex's van and I'll never see you again."

She stepped out of the truck as the teens walked off,

laughing. One had thrown a can towards Murgatroyd, and left a cigarette burning on the ground, not even bothering to step it out. Lyra felt her face flaming with anger.

She saw that Alex had come out of his truck to protect and comfort Murgatroyd, so she veered off and went to the waterline, stooping down to see if she could grab the two beer cans bobbing there. She managed to fetch one out, but the other was too far from reach.

An arm reached out past hers and grabbed the can. Lyra stood up too quickly, feeling giddy from the lack of blood in her head. Alex put a hand on her shoulder to steady her.

"Thanks," she mumbled, embarrassed. They were standing very close to one another, and he was looking down at her with an unreadable expression on his face.

"You were coming out to check on Murgatroyd." She nodded. "Thank you."

"It's not a big deal." His hand was still on her shoulder and she was very conscious of it. She took a deep breath and collected herself, stepping back from his grasp for the second time that day. He let his hand fall slowly, still looking at her.

"But as you can see," she added, "this is no place for the poor fellow. He should probably go back to a farm."

Alex shook his head and she felt a spike of irritation. If he was trying to ruin them, she found his way of warfare even creepier than what they'd faced in the city - because some-times it felt like true friendliness.

She shrugged and headed back to the truck, dropping the beer can into the garbage bin on the way.

CHAPTER ELEVEN

"I'm sorry I haven't finished the song I started writing for you," Lyra said to Mick as they stood fiddling with their equipment in his small garage before a Saturday afternoon rehearsal session.

Mick wore a check shirt with the sleeves customised to show off his wound. It was healing well and he told Lyra it made him feel chosen. She understood completely. If she had a scar like that you could hardly have made her wear clothes again.

"I love the idea." He smiled at her. "It's the nicest thing anyone's ever thought about doing for me."

"We need to get you some better friends."

He laughed. Lyra knew the reasons she clung to Mick and didn't want to replace him, no matter what Silas said. But she was never quite sure of the reasons he was so steadfastly loyal to her, although she suspected that he felt a little sorry for her. Whenever Lyra brought up the topic, Mick shrugged and told her he knew she was headed for big things, and he was serving himself by hanging onto her coattails.

No one knew her voice and moods like he did, no one got

the sound exactly right like he did, no one improvised in the delightful, surprising way he did. Lyra loved every second of their time together.

As they launched into their first song, Lyra felt that way again. Transported. Singing and music made her feel like she belonged to another world. One where anything was possible. Where there was dark and light in equal measure, but above everything else there was a sense of power and agency. It was a world where she was completely in control.

That feeling gave her goosebumps. Lyra knew she had a great voice. Perhaps she didn't have star power or maybe her songs weren't always radio-worthy, but she did often catch Silas humming one or another of them, and then claiming it wasn't hers. She was confident that her best songs were well above mediocre.

The idea that she could one day do this full time...well it scared as much as thrilled her. *What if the magic disappears when you get to live your dreams?* She had written once in her diary. *What if the power that kept them going was the knowledge, you'd have to keep fighting for them the rest of your life?*

Lyra was lost in a high note when Mick's keyboard blew out, for no apparent reason.

"Huh." He examined the smoking plug. "Knock me down with a feather."

"Do you think you can fix it before our gig at Rusty's Pub?" she asked anxiously.

"Sure can. I'll get Harry to take a look at it later today."

"Great. Well...then I guess it's time for a break."

She pulled two beers from the small fridge and popped the tops off. They rolled up the garage door and sat at the white plastic table and chairs, letting the mild breeze flow in.

Mick's phone rang and he looked at the screen, then swiped to reject the call.

"My brother," he said tonelessly and took a swig.

Lyra didn't know where she stood in this strange territory. She knew Mick's wife leaving him for his brother earlier this year was a deep wound that would never really heal, but was it something she should get him to talk about, or rather leave alone? She had known Mick's wife, of course, but had never really been close to her.

"You...don't speak to your brother anymore?" she asked tentatively.

Mick shrugged. "What am I going to say?"

"She's an idiot, by the way. For leaving you, I mean."

"It's never that easy."

"Isn't it?"

"They had their reasons. You can't hang on to someone if they don't want to be with you. It's like trying to catch the wind." His eyes had a faraway look in them.

"But why didn't they tell you when they first started to have feelings for each other? Isn't it always best to be honest?"

He sighed heavily, like he had given this a lot of thought. "Nothing can grow when it's announced so early and watched so closely. Maybe they weren't sure yet." He took a sip of his beer.

"I hate her."

"That's a waste of time. Hurts no one but you."

"You're so zen, Mick! I wouldn't be able to do it. Unless..." She looked sidelong at him, uncertain whether or not to voice the question niggling in the back of her mind. Had he cheated on her first?

He seemed to sense what she was thinking and quickly changed the subject.

"How's Silas?" He said it casually, but there was an edge to his voice. Imperceptible probably to anyone other than Lyra, but she could detect the strained note.

"He's good," she said slowly. "Did something happen between you two? He's been a bit...off lately."

Mick looked the other way, not saying anything for a while. "Your brother has a lot of scars to heal," he said quietly. "Be gentle with him, Lyra."

He got up for a bathroom break, making clear the conversation was over. Lyra nodded, but felt as though there was a piece of some puzzle that she was missing.

CHAPTER TWELVE

Later that evening, Lyra met the girls at the Whistle Stop.

"So," Amy said, as soon as the three of them were seated around the barrel and had cold drinks in their hands. "How's it working out with Margot?"

Marley turned to Lyra, eager for the news.

"Good! Actually, better than good. I've had two email inquiries already. That's two more than I ever got when my name was out there alone."

"Is Mick ready for the gig on Saturday?" Amy asked.

"Well, aside from the fact that his keyboard blew out." Marley groaned. "Which he says he can fix quickly," Lyra added, "he's in pretty good shape."

"Well, we'll both be there obviously," Marley said.

"And did you do what I said about answering the phone without a name and being whoever they ask for?" Amy asked.

"Yep!" They clinked glasses and Lyra took a sip of her drink, feeling very pleased with herself. She also noticed that her eyes were casting around involuntarily for Miles.

"He's here, don't worry," Amy said in a low voice.

"How...?"

"Rick knows one of the guys who works here. I asked him to discreetly find out."

"Wait, Shy Boy is called Rick? How have you not told us that already?"

"I'm telling you everything now." Amy smiled coyly. "He works in construction..." she arched an eyebrow, "so the stamina level is very high."

Marley giggled behind her hand.

"And?" Lyra prompted.

"And..." she hesitated and put her drink down and took a deep breath as though she was about to say something momentous. "Girls...I think I might really like him."

Marley squealed and hugged her.

"Amy Porter." Lyra shook her head and pretended to be disappointed. She was completely unable to hide a grin. "Who'd have guessed you'd ever fall for someone?"

"Well, he's not just anyone." Amy smiled.

"So when are we all going to be properly introduced?" Lyra asked.

"I'm going to bring him to the gig on Saturday, if that's okay?"

"Are you kidding? That would be awesome! Now I have an extra reason to look forward to it."

"Speaking of falling for someone..." Amy said in a low voice and raised her eyebrow.

"Hey, ladies." Miles was suddenly close to Lyra's ear. He leaned towards her, torso lightly touching her shoulder, and pressed his hands onto the barrel top. Lyra could smell his smoky strawberry scent and see his biceps flexing through his shirt. "What are you up to tonight?"

Her mind instantly vacated and she could think of

nothing amusing to say. Nothing to say at all. Amy gestured for Miles to sit down.

"Can't - gotta stay on the move, but just thought I'd come and see if I could get you anything special?" He winked at Lyra.

After another awkward silence, Amy spoke up. "Round of shots, please. I think we all need them."

"Coming right up!" he said and sauntered away.

"Wow," Marley said as soon as he was gone. "You really clam up when he's around."

"Yes. Thank you, Marley, for pointing that out."

She sipped her drink and surveyed Lyra. "But I mean, you really go to pieces. He's not going to like you if you never say a single thing to him."

Lyra looked helplessly at Amy, who shrugged. "She's right. You've got to pull yourself together. He's just a dumb guy."

Lyra felt they were ganging up on her. She had no tactics for "pulling herself together" in situations like this. She didn't even really know what the problem was. Miles wasn't the most beautiful guy in the world or anything. She wasn't even sure yet if she felt a sense of connection with him. But he *was* cute, and he seemed at least mildly interested. Maybe she was also interested in him? One thing was for sure, she would never find out if she couldn't get her act together and open her mouth.

"Just pretend he's ugly and you don't care," Amy said. "That's what always works for me."

"Oh, look. There's another musician setting up," Marley said. Lyra and Amy turned to look.

Miles was standing beside a leggy redhead in a short black leather skirt as she set up her microphone on the corner stage. She threw her head back to laugh at something he said and the sound floated over to them, throaty and full. Lyra felt her face burning.

The woman leaned towards Miles and whispered something in his ear. It was his turn to burst out laughing.

"That's what you've got to do," Marley said helpfully. "Make him laugh like that. Wow. He really finds her funny. They have really good chemistry."

Lyra shot Amy a look that clearly said Marley had better watch herself in dark alleys and Amy steered the conversation in a safer direction.

"What about you, Marley," she asked. "Anyone in your sights?"

Marley turned to her and sighed heavily. "Honestly, I feel like I'm still getting to know myself after my move to Sydney. I've always wanted to try a one-night stand, but I really don't think I could go through with it. A relationship just isn't a priority for me right now." She shrugged again and studied the menu.

In another person, this might have been reluctance to share, or a show of bravado. With Marley, it was the truth. She was so candid with her thoughts and feelings and so happy to expose her vulnerabilities that Lyra found it heroic. She admired her and tried to learn from her. Even while sometimes wanting to strangle her.

Miles returned with a tray of shots for them, declaring with a little wink at Lyra that they were on the house. Marley ordered Buffalo Wings.

Four shots later, Lyra was finally finding her voice in Miles's presence. She wasn't exactly on fire, but nor was she clamming up anymore when he made his ever more frequent visits to their table. His attention was always half-fixed on the redhead singing, but something about that spurred Lyra on now instead of intimidating her.

Right now, he'd stopped at their table to deliver Marley's

wings, and had his hand on Lyra's leg as Amy asked him about the whiskey tasting sessions at the Whistle Stop. Lyra found herself studying the hand on her leg. Was it rude that he was touching her without asking? Alex had touched her arm, but that had somehow felt different.

A few tables down from them, the mousy barmaid who'd stared at Lyra when she gave Miles her number, was serving a table of rowdy young men. One of the them smacked her on the behind as she walked away with their order, jerking her forward.

"Don't you *touch* Eliza," Miles yelled, immediately leaving the girls. He marched over to the table and loudly threatened to have security remove the boys if they didn't apologise. They all mumbled something more or less under their breath, but they did it.

Lyra's heart swelled a little watching the scene. She and Amy smiled at one another, and then Miles went over to Eliza and slipped his arm around her shoulders. She leaned gratefully into him, almost as if he was a lifeline. It was obvious he enjoyed the admiration.

Lyra frowned.

"He's just taken her under his wing," Amy said. "That's all."

Lyra raised half a smile. Marley caught the tail end of the exchange, looking up at them and nodding.

"Although," she said, holding up a finger in thought, "I have always wondered why they're called buffalo wings at all?"

Lyra and Amy laughed, but Lyra's awkwardness wasn't quite so quick to dissolve.

When the red headed singer stopped for an interval in her set, Miles weaved his way through the crowd towards her. He was cut off by a bulky, tall man in a leather jacket, who scooped the redhead into his arms and kissed her passionately. Her boyfriend, obviously. This triggered a surge of relief in Lyra. The redhead wasn't her competition, even if her music had been tolerable.

Miles awkwardly said something to the pair of them, and then went to the bar to fetch them drinks. The whole encounter left Lyra flushed with triumph, but seemed to embarrass Amy.

An hour or so later, the girls were ready to call it a night. Amy wanted a head start on an early meeting with a new client and Marley felt queasy after the wings. Lyra tried to hide her disappointment as she kissed them both goodbye and headed to the bathroom before her walk home. She was washing her hands when she looked up at the mirror, shocked to see Miles reflected behind her. She spun and the grin on his face widened.

"Gotcha," he said. "I was hoping I hadn't missed you."

Lyra's heart was pounding, mostly from fright. "Well, here I am," she said, somewhat lamely, holding her arms out.

He took a step closer and she felt her pulse start to quicken. It seemed a little sudden of him to make a move now...they'd barely spoken and she hadn't exactly set the world on fire during those times. She knew absolutely nothing about him, aside from the fact that he looked good and had chivalrously saved Eliza.

"Is there anyone else in here?" he whispered.

Lyra shook her head. He took another step towards her, and she breathed in his heady scent. His hair was perfectly mussed and she noticed for the first time he had a small silver hoop through the cartilage of his ear. He was definitely a good-looking guy, and if this was a sign he was interested in Lyra...she could do worse.

"How's Eliza doing?" She hated that her voice came out

sounding slightly nervous as Miles took another step towards her.

"Oh, she's fine. Those guys were idiots. They needed to be taught a lesson." Lyra nodded. "I've seen you watching me," Miles continued and closed the gap between them. Her heart rate increased and she felt warmth flooding her face. "Do you like me, Lyra?"

It was a strange question to ask, but she considered it before nodding slowly. She *did* like him, or at least, she was attracted to him and wanted to get to know more about him.

Miles was so close to her now that she could feel the heat from his body. Very, very slowly, with their eyes locked together, he leaned in to kiss her. She kissed him back tentatively, waiting to be swept away on a tide of lust.

These sorts of stolen rendezvous were the kind of thing that happened in the novels her stepmother had kept a secret stash of in a box marked "Bibles & misc." under her twin bed in the room she shared with Lyra's father. It was the stuff that had made Lyra tingle when she was younger and reading it, feeling the first little flutters of longing. Somehow, it felt different living it in real life. She couldn't say it was disappointing exactly, but...neither was she feeling carried away.

They heard footsteps heading towards the bathroom and Miles pulled quickly away, breaking off their kiss. He coughed loudly and straightened his clothes then, with a quick smile thrown casually over his shoulder, he was gone before the person entered.

The footsteps belonged to Eliza. She stood in the doorway and looked down the hall at Miles' receding form, then back at Lyra. Her eyes narrowed slightly and she took a moment to choose her words.

"Did something just happen between you two?" Lyra didn't see how that was any of her business. She turned to the wash basin again and Eliza glared at her in the reflection. "Well, did it?" Eliza asked again.

"I don't really want to talk about it with you," Lyra said. The whole situation was odd and unsettling.

Eliza nodded once. "Well, you should know that he's not looking for a girlfriend right now." There was a note of bitterness in her voice. "And if I were you, I wouldn't go around thinking you're different or special."

Lyra brushed past her and didn't turn back.

CHAPTER THIRTEEN

On the night of Lyra and Mick's gig at Rusty's Pub, Lyra chose her outfit carefully. It had been a while since she'd been in front of a crowd and she wanted to dress for power and confidence. She decided on a simple black slip dress made of a kind of shimmery material, with her hair loose and wavy. She dug around in her side of the bathroom cupboard until she found her single tube of lipstick - a bright red that she only wore on-stage.

Standing in front of the bathroom mirror, she opened her phone and scrolled to Miles's number. *Mick and I are playing tonight at Rusty's. See you there?* she wrote, adding a map pin to the message. She shook her head and backspaced until it was gone. Too presumptuous.

You off work tonight? she tried again, but then worried it sounded like an invitation for a booty call. She deleted that too. *My manager got a gig for us tonight at Rusty's,* she typed. *Stop by if you're free.* She hit send before she could second guess it and put her phone face down on the counter.

She was still unsettled from the encounter with Eliza in the bathroom a week earlier. The fact there'd basically been radio silence from Miles since the kiss didn't help either. Lyra hated feeling like this. Insecure and uncertain where she stood. It was unsettling. As was the fact that she often found Alex on her mind...

"You're wearing *that*?" Silas asked her, leaning on the door jamb as she fussed with her hair in the mirror. She looked at his reflection. He was grinning and she knew that meant he approved of her outfit. She blew him a kiss.

"How are we getting there?" he asked.

"Mick's driving."

Lyra saw a look of absolute horror flash across his face and couldn't help laughing.

"Just kidding!" she said and his eyes narrowed. "We're getting a taxi, Mick's getting a lift there with the equipment."

Silas breathed an exaggerated sigh of relief and then hit her on the shoulder. "For a moment, I thought our loving father would have to read our obituaries in the paper." He walked over to the mirror and palmed his perfect hair this way and that. He looked incredible, as usual.

"You think he'd recognise our names?" Lyra asked. It was an old wound and deep, but they'd found a way to joke around and it made a kind of peace with the way things were.

"I mean, we have unusual names so there's a good chance. But who really knows. It depends on where the good Lord is guiding him that day."

As they left the bathroom, they passed a framed picture of their mother holding the two of them as small children. They had been so excited when they could finally afford to live together just the two of them, that one of the first things they'd done was hang up framed photos of their mother. Lyra kissed her fingers and pressed them onto the glass of the photo, the way she always did when she passed it.

"Right," she said, tugging at the hemline of her dress and

readjusting the shoulder straps. "Pour me some courage, please."

"I'm not sure that's a good idea."

"Please." Lyra made big eyes at him, which she knew he could never resist.

He turned to scan their sparse drinks shelf. "Mexican or Irish?"

"We don't have any Russian?" she asked hopefully.

"No vodka, sorry,"

"Okay, then…tequila."

"But remember what happened last time?"

"That was a one-off." Lyra tried to reach past him for the bottle.

He blocked her and looked her in the eyes. "Lyra, I found you naked in a shopping trolley in the back yard with no idea how you got there."

"Like I said-"

"You want to do that on stage?"

She slumped in defeat. "I guess I'll have a whiskey."

"Actually, remember-"

"Okay, this is ridiculous! Don't we have some white wine or something?"

At that moment a car horn honked.

"Too late!" Silas said. "That's the cab. Out you scoot."

He pushed her away from the drinks cabinet, grabbed her handbag and led her out the door.

Rusty's was already crowded as Lyra and Silas arrived at the same time as Amy and Mick. Shortly afterward, Amy spotted Rick and Lyra saw his face light up as they walked towards each other. It made Lyra smile. Rick looked like the kind of guy she could see Amy with long term.

Rusty walked over to them, casting his eyes around, obviously looking for something.

"Margot here?" he asked, hopefully.

Lyra was dumbstruck. She'd assumed Amy would fill him in on the real situation. She turned to Mick for help, her mouth opening and closing.

"She couldn't make it unfortunately, mate," Mick said smoothly, stepping forward to shake Rusty's hand. "Mick. Lesser half of this operation." Rusty nodded and shook his hand politely, doing a relatively good job of hiding his disappointment.

"Why don't you all get set up over there?" He jerked his thumb in the direction of a small stage.

Silas helped haul some of the equipment over as Lyra saw Marley arrive and horn her way in on Amy and Rick's obviously intimate conversation. As she and Silas wove through the crowd, Lyra heard a sharp intake of breath. She turned and saw a cute but slightly gangly-looking guy staring at Silas.

"Cheer real loud and I'll introduce you," she whispered to him with a wink.

He grinned. "I'm Ernie." He shot his hand out and Lyra shook it, laughing.

"Lyra. Pleased to meet you, future brother-in-law." Ernie turned back to his friend, who winked at her in thanks and slapped Ernie's shoulder encouragingly.

Lyra quickly checked her phone to see whether Miles had replied to her text yet. The message was marked as read, but there was still no response. Lyra knew the chances were slim that he could make it, he likely had to work, but it felt like something he should at least reply to. She told herself he was probably just busy and would message later.

As they headed towards the stage with their gear in tow,

there was a loud cackle from a group of men all dressed in tracksuits.

"Great," one of them said sneeringly, waving around a beer glass that definitely wasn't his first. "Some two-bit chick and her grandpa are here to entertain us."

"Three-bit, thanks," Lyra said.

"Wey-hey! She bites!" he said. His friends slapped their thighs along with him. "Can't wait to see what you and Pops have in store for us, love."

"You just settle in and pretend it's your living room," Lyra said, in her sweetest voice. "Since you're already dressed like it is."

She heard them explode into laughter, cat-calling as she rolled her eyes. Mick grinned and shot her a thumbs up for her comeback.

They spent a few moments tuning up and getting ready, then just before they began their set, Lyra sneaked a last look at her phone. Miles had texted back. One word. *Cool.*

Her heart sank. It felt dismissive and cold and she found it totally at odds with the way he had approached and kissed her in the bathroom. She really had no idea where they stood, what they were, what they had any chance of becoming. But there was no time to ponder any of that now. She needed all her attention for the stage.

She resolutely switched her phone off, tossing it into one of the bags behind Mick, and grabbed the mic.

"Hi, everyone," she said, and the din quietened just a little. "Thanks for coming this evening, and thanks to Rusty for having us."

A huge, wild cheer went up. Silas, Amy, Rick, Marley and even Ernie were making enough noise for the whole bar.

"A big thanks to our fans, as well." She grinned. "I'm Lyra, this is Mick, and we're about to sing you some songs."

The first three songs went beautifully. Some people

danced, some talked, some just sat and listened, swaying to the music. There was a feeling of harmony and peace within her, which felt mirrored through the room. She forgot all about her inner turmoil over Miles and was completely in the moment.

Just as she launched into one of their big crowd favourite original songs, she locked eyes with Alex. She was surprised to see him there and felt slightly unsteady as she continued with the song.

She started to panic as they headed to the chorus, unable to recall the words although she'd sung them so many times. She felt her face reddening with a sense of horror that she was going to mess up. She looked at Alex again. He was staring at her with a strange look in his eyes and a half-smile on his lips.

She scanned the room in search of something else to focus on - Amy and Rick furiously making out in the corner, with Marley still trying to hold a conversation with them. Ernie, who was so obviously smitten with Silas that he was staring at him right now. And finally Silas himself, standing tall and confident and beautiful in the corner of the room, ignoring every single thing in the world but her. He smiled at her and nodded gently and the words suddenly came flooding in.

Lyra hit the notes perfectly and felt the room fall silent. She tingled the way she always did when things were going right. The transported feeling. The best feeling she'd ever experienced in the world.

As Mick played the final chords and a round of applause kicked up, there was a sudden commotion in front of the stage. Two of the track-suited men were shoving one another, bumping into a table behind them, spilling drinks and upsetting people.

Silas, who knew how to handle himself in a fight, started

heading over to them. But Rusty was quicker, breaking them up effortlessly. For a relatively small older man, Rusty had a commanding and pugnacious presence. The way the group fell instantly into line told Lyra he'd probably needed to take them on before. And that he'd won.

"We're going to take a quick break, folks, so grab a drink and we'll see you back here soon!" she said into the mic.

As she stepped down from the stage and headed toward Silas, Alex cut her path off.

"Lyra." His eyes were shining. "That was..."

"What are you doing here?" Her voice came out sharper than she'd intended, especially since the surprise wasn't altogether unwelcome. She quickly tried to turn it into a joke. "Are you following us?"

"Calm down, sis," Silas said, joining them. "He probably had no idea you were going to be here."

"Hey, Silas." Alex clapped him on the shoulder and turned back to Lyra, holding her gaze. "I knew. I often come to Rusty's and I saw it on their website. I was just curious, that's all."

Silas nodded, not looking entirely convinced.

"How are we doing?" Lyra asked Silas. She always looked forward to his feedback on their sets. He was honest and critical, but not brutal.

"What do you think, Alex?" Silas asked. Lyra felt her heart rate pick up as Alex smiled.

"I thought it was..." he groped for the words, not taking his eyes off her. "Magical," he said finally, and she found herself blushing.

Lyra tried unsuccessfully to hide a smile, then looked around, full of a strange energy that she wasn't quite sure what to do with.

"Thank you. I need to find Mick." She spun on her heel.

Then everything happened at once.

Ernie, carrying two beers in his hands and a beaming smile on his face, was headed toward Silas, excited about his introduction. Also heading toward them from a slightly different angle was Mick - not facing the direction he was walking in.

"Look out!" Lyra yelled in panic, but her voice was swallowed by the crowd and then it was too late.

In slow motion, Mick and Ernie collided heavily. Mick pitched sideways, smashed his mouth onto a nearby table and went down, face bloodied. He tried to catch himself on the table, but only succeeded in dragging it over, sending glasses and drinks crashing to the floor right beside the tracksuit men, who assumed they were under attack and started swinging at the innocent patrons of the tipped-over table, who were bewildered as to what had happened.

A mortified Ernie bent down to help Mick but one of the glasses slipped from his hand, smashing beside Mick's face. The glass exploded and Mick was soaked with beer, small cuts instantly appearing on his cheek. A barmaid rushed over, slipped on the spilled beer and landed heavily on top of Mick, her leg bent at an awkward angle.

Lyra, Silas and Alex turned to each other in absolute horror and hurried to form a protective ring around Mick and the barmaid as the brawl - now in full swing - lurched towards their prostrate figures.

CHAPTER FOURTEEN

R ick drove Amy and Lyra to the hospital in his car. Lyra was briefly allowed to see Mick, who looked better once his cuts had been cleaned up. He'd needed one stitch above his lip, but that was thankfully all. They were keeping him in for observation, but Lyra knew he'd be fine. He'd survived much worse. The barmaid had unfortunately broken her leg.

Lyra said goodnight to Mick and headed back to the hospital entrance, where Amy and Rick were waiting for her.

Amy was dragging heavily on a cigarette and Rick looked pained as he watched her do it. She'd quit years ago, but said she needed one tonight. Lyra wasn't about to argue with her, she almost wanted one herself. Her hands hadn't stopped shaking since the incident and now it was being made worse by the evening's chill. She regretted not having brought a jacket.

"So, when do you think Rusty will book us to play again?" she joked uneasily to Amy.

Lyra couldn't even estimate the damage that had been done to Rusty's bar. Along with Mick and the barmaid, two patrons and one of the track-suited men had been admitted to hospital. Lyra just hoped they kept everyone in separate rooms.

Amy choked out a humourless laugh. "I'll ask him."

"Seriously, Amy," Lyra said, "I am so, so-"

"Oh no, it's not your fault! I just hated seeing that much blood. I'm not smoking because I'm mad at you or the situation. Little known fact," she added, turning to Rick as she stubbed out her cigarette into a small pail filled with sand, "I look tough but blood and violence are two things I absolutely *cannot* stand."

Lyra thought Rick looked a little awkward with that admission and more awkward still when Amy wrapped her arms tightly around his waist and murmured, "Thank goodness you work in construction."

"Right. Because there's never been an accident in construction." He smiled tightly.

Lyra knew she'd still have to go back to Rusty's and collect all the gear at some point, but for now, Rusty had agreed to keep it until Mick's medical situation was clear.

Amy turned to Lyra suddenly. "Oh, I meant to ask you. Who was the dish you were talking to when...everything happened?"

"Huh?"

"Tall guy? Dark hair?"

"Oh! That's Alex. The guy who runs the food truck next to us."

"Honey, you need to get over yourself and get started on him."

Lyra flushed. "I don't even know what he was doing there. Besides, Miles..."

"Miles Schmiles. I know what Alex was doing there. I saw the way he was looking at you!"

Lyra felt uneasy with the direction the conversation had

taken. "You didn't see anything except the back of Rick's throat," she said and Amy grinned.

Lyra rubbed her upper arms with her hands to warm them and made a mental note to start packing a shawl or jacket in the evenings now. The weather was definitely turning.

"Amy, I have to head off," Rick said. "I have an early start tomorrow."

"I won't kiss you because I smoked, but I'll see you soon."

Rick bent over and wrapped her tightly in a hug, closing his eyes as he held her. The emotion on his face was so naked, Lyra had to turn away.

"Sorry about the throat comment," she said to him. He grinned to let her know it was okay and then headed off. Amy didn't see it, but he turned back twice to look at her.

"Speaking of Alex..." Amy's eyes were fixed on something over Lyra's shoulder. Lyra swatted her.

"Don't joke about things like that!"

"Hi, Lyra."

She froze, her eyes widening at Amy, who was grinning. Lyra spun to face Alex. He'd stuffed his hands into the pockets of his jeans, which she was beginning to realise was his nervous gesture, and he was wearing a knitted cardigan that he hadn't had on at Rusty's.

The cardigan was thick and warm-looking, definitely hand-made. It made Lyra's insides feel soft to imagine a grandma or aunt had knitted it for him and he wore it with pride. Ernie was standing beside Alex, looking sheepish.

"What are you doing here?" Lyra asked.

They answered simultaneously.

"I wanted to apologise to Mick, and see if Silas was here..." Ernie stammered, as Alex said, "I just wanted to make sure everyone was fine."

"Everyone, huh?" Amy asked Alex pointedly. He flicked

his eyes towards her, instantly recognizing a kindred spirit. Lyra noticed that his grey-gold eyes were lit up by the hospital lights, making them look huge and deep, and that the thin silver thread of an old scar ran from his lip down to his chin. For a moment, she imagined what it would be like to run her fingers over the scar and pull that mouth to hers. She coughed and drew a sharp breath, turning to Ernie.

"I'm really sorry," she said, "Silas didn't come to the hospital. He went home to get a good night's rest because he's manning our food truck alone tomorrow."

"You two run a food truck?" Ernie asked, sounding awed.

"It's a good one, too," Alex said, and Lyra shot him a puzzled look.

"I can pass on your number?" she suggested to Ernie. "Although...I'm not sure he knows who you are yet, sorry."

"I'm the guy that almost killed your band member," Ernie said sadly. He looked so downcast that Alex patted him on the shoulder and the two of them stared as Lyra and Amy burst into laughter.

"What's so funny?" Ernie asked finally, sounded wounded.

"If you knew what Mick had survived, this year alone-" Alex looked confused. Ernie seemed so forlorn Lyra wanted to hug him. "No one can kill Mick. That wasn't even the best attempt this month." Ernie looked sceptical. "I'd take you in right now to prove it, but visiting hours are done. We were all just out here to say goodnight and decompress. But I promise you, Mick isn't going anywhere. He's absolutely fine."

Ernie nodded, not looking quite convinced. A silence fell and Lyra wasn't quite sure what to say. Amy read the moment, gave Lyra a quick hug and kiss goodnight, and hooked her arm through Ernie's.

"I'll give you directions to my place, thanks for the lift

home," she said to him, as she steered him towards the car park.

"Sure." Ernie nodded, waving at Alex and Lyra as he walked away, not entirely sure what had just happened.

Alex stuffed his hands into his pockets and they stood awkwardly for a moment.

"Lyra, I meant what I said at the show," he said in a low voice. "I think you're incredible. Your voice, I mean," he added hastily.

"Thank you." She was annoyed at how much his words pleased her. "How's Murgatroyd?"

Alex laughed. Lyra liked the sound of it - warm and genuine. Wordlessly, he pulled off his cardigan and draped it over her shoulders. She hadn't realised she'd still been hugging them. The cardigan was already warm with his body heat, and instantly she let go of the tension she'd been holding in her body. She should refuse it, she knew. But it was soft and Alex didn't look cold.

"Thank you." She pulled the sides of the cardigan tightly around herself. It smelled the same as Alex - laundry soap and the slightest hint of cologne.

"Murgatroyd's fine. He'll be back tomorrow and he'll be very pleased you asked about him."

She smiled. She wanted to ask Alex about his plans with the food truck. Why he was playing such hardball at times during the day and then behaving like this right afterwards? Although, when she thought about it, his behaviour hadn't really changed since they'd met him. It had mostly been that stupid sandwich board, but that had done him more harm than good.

Lyra was willing to admit she might have been projecting her fears on him, punishing him for the things she and Silas had been through in the city. It was a strange thought, but she wasn't quite ready to let her guard down yet.

"Do you need a lift home?" Alex asked. "Or is your boyfriend coming to pick you up?"

Lyra opened and closed her mouth. Miles was anything but a boyfriend. He hadn't followed up his text with anything else, hadn't asked how their set had gone, or whether she was doing anything later. It almost seemed as though she didn't exist for Miles unless she was right there at the bar.

Still, they'd kissed. She wasn't sure it meant anything to her, but she didn't want to go around starting anything else before she figured that out. She blushed, suddenly realising she was getting completely carried away with herself. Alex wasn't asking for her hand in marriage, he was asking whether she wanted a ride home.

She nodded. "He's not coming, so a lift would be great, thanks. If it's not out of your way."

"You live in the food truck, right?" he said and they both grinned.

"That's right. The whole thing folds out into a two-room flat when you press a button in the back. It's really convenient."

They were still laughing when a familiar voice cut through the evening air.

"Alex?"

They turned to the entrance and saw Alison, staring at them in confusion.

"Alison?" Lyra said, taking a few steps towards her. "How's Mick doing? Have you finished your shift? And how do you know…?"

Lyra suddenly thought of Alison crying, telling her she'd cheated on her boyfriend and was moving out. Alex saying *all's fair in love and war,* with that strange look in his eyes on the day he'd first parked the truck at Lilac Bay. A crazy *what if* crossed Lyra's mind and made her stomach lurch.

She looked quickly to Alex to see whether her hunch was

right. He was looking at Alison with wide eyes, his face ashen.

"Alex." Alison looked straight through Lyra as though she wasn't there. "It is *so* good to see you."

She took a few steps toward him and he took a step back. Lyra felt suddenly and embarrassingly like the third wheel. They obviously needed privacy, didn't need her standing there staring at them. She took a few steps backward as Alison closed the gap between her and Alex. Neither of them seemed to notice Lyra.

A taxi dropped someone off at the doors and flicked its light to vacant.

"I'm going to grab a cab," Lyra said softly, wondering whether Alex would notice. His eyes were still fixed on Alison's. Alison hadn't even acknowledged Lyra.

She waved to the taxi and got in, giving the driver her address as she closed the door. No one stopped her. As they drove slowly past Alison and Alex, Lyra could see that they were locked in an intense conversation. Alison was gesturing broadly and pleadingly and Alex's face was stony, his jaw tight.

Lyra realised she was still wearing Alex's cardigan and something about that made her want to cry. Her fingers strayed to her mother's gold locket.

She missed her mother painfully at that moment. Mothers were always supposed to know what to say to make you feel better. It wasn't fair she didn't have hers anymore.

CHAPTER FIFTEEN

Halfway into the following week, Alex and Lyra still hadn't spoken. Lyra had his cardigan and knew she needed to give it back, but often found herself wearing it in the evenings at home. She told herself she'd wash it and bring it back to him soon. He hadn't asked for it in any case. They'd waved, and exchanged quick smiles if they happened to catch eyes, but that was it. Lyra wasn't sure how to ask about things with Alison and knew it wasn't any of her business in any case.

She got the feeling Alex was avoiding her, but couldn't be sure. As a distraction, she took her phone out and studied her text message history with Miles. He'd sent one at 2am that morning. *What are you up to? ;)*

Lyra hadn't responded, because she wasn't entirely sure he'd meant to send it to her. And, at 2am, surely there was only one response he hoped to get from a message like that. She sighed, and tucked the phone into her back pocket. Why was romance always so complicated?

"How are the vegetable pies selling?" she asked Silas.

He glared at her. "You own this place too, in case you forgot. How do you think they're selling?"

Lyra avoided answering, instead looking out at Murgatroyd in his pen. Alex had put up a small sun umbrella to shade him, careful that it didn't obstruct the lamb's view of the water. As usual, there was a small crowd gathered around the pen.

"You're distracted as heck, Lyra. You've given out three wrong orders today and undercharged about five people."

Her shoulders slumped. She knew he was right. She hadn't really been paying that much attention the last couple of days.

"What's going on?" he asked her, this time more tenderly.

"I guess it's guy trouble?"

Silas groaned. "Are you still on about that guy from the bar?"

She shrugged. "Maybe?" She started organising the snack foods as Silas watched her closely, his arms folded.

"Well, what about him?"

"We kissed a while ago, and I get the odd text, but...he feels indifferent."

"So be indifferent back."

"Well, then it will just completely fizzle."

"Then maybe it's supposed to."

Lyra let the words sink in, then changed the subject. "Did you go visit Mick yet?" Mick had been released the morning after the fight and Lyra had already been to check on him and reassure herself he was fine.

Now it was Silas's turn to look busy and avoid her gaze. He shook his head.

A teenage couple holding hands arrived at the window and asked for directions to the Secret Garden. Lyra pointed them towards the spot, which was set back off the sandy beach within the hook of the bay. They bought a drink and a pie to share before heading on their way.

"Why haven't you visited him?" Lyra asked as soon as they left.

"Lyra, I'm really busy at the moment."

She put her hands on her hips. "Okay, what is going on between the two of you? You've been avoiding him and he's saying strange things about you and I don't really understand when we stopped being family."

Silas looked up. "What's he said about me?"

Lyra tried to remember the exact words. "That you have scars that need to heal, I think."

Silas made a face but said nothing further.

"Can you *please* tell me what's going on?" Silas was silent for a moment, then reached out and lifted their mother's locket from under Lyra's shirt.

"You wear this every day?" He rubbed his thumb over it gently.

She nodded. "What's that got to do with anything?"

Silas smiled tightly and dropped the locket back down. "Nothing." He turned away. It felt like a window had closed on the topic.

Lyra sighed and they both silently went about their tasks. They took turns serving customers, then, on her break, Lyra decided to head to the Secret Garden. The teens had reminded her of it and she felt drawn to the place in her current mood.

T he Secret Garden had been imagined into life by a prominent artist who still lived in the area. She'd started off just caring for the ancient, gnarled fig trees. Then she'd built twisting, turning pathways among the trees, coaxed thousands of plants to life, and integrated artwork and sculpture into the landscape over the years.

Her husband's and daughter's ashes had been scattered within the garden's boundaries. It was a magical place, so close to the city and yet it felt isolated and hushed. Lyra's mind slowly cleared as she wandered through. It felt like a good place to remember people and Lyra's mother had been on her mind a lot lately.

She strolled slowly back to the food truck and was surprised to find Alex's truck shuttered. He must have decided to leave early.

"Did you ever call Ernie?" she asked Silas as she tied her apron back on.

Silas frowned. "The skinny guy from Rusty's?" She nodded. "No."

"Why not? What do you have to lose?"

Silas shrugged. "He really isn't my type. I like..." His gaze wandered almost involuntarily to Meat is Murder.

Lyra felt a spike of irritation. "You've got someone who'd crawl on broken glass just to meet with you and you're throwing yourself at a straight guy."

"Okay, *one*," Silas said, putting a hand on his hip as the other looped sassily through the air till he held a single finger right in her face, "the glass is broken because Ernie *broke it himself*. And two, if you think this is throwing myself at someone, you need to go back to the nunnery."

They glared at each other for a moment until the humour of his words struck her. Her mouth twitched, then his did, and soon they'd collapsed into giggles.

"The heart wants what the heart wants," he said a moment later, unconsciously echoing Mick's sentiments. "Besides. I don't want to burst your bubble, but there's not a tonne of evidence this Miles guy is into you, either."

CHAPTER SIXTEEN

Silas's words had got her thinking, more than she was
willing to admit. She called Amy and Marley and
asked them whether they wanted to meet up at the
Whistle Stop that evening. Amy was fresh back from a long
weekend with Rick so Lyra wasn't sure she'd feel like an
evening out, but both girls quickly agreed.

Lyra was going to conduct an experiment with Miles.
Eliza's words kept echoing in her mind: *He's not looking for a
girlfriend right now.* How would Eliza know that, unless she'd
asked or tried something with him, or vice versa.

Was Lyra looking for a boyfriend? She never really
thought too much about her relationship status, but she did
hope to find someone, yes. Was it Miles? That seemed
unlikely. But she hadn't been able to stop thinking about
their kiss. Not so much how good it had felt, although it had
felt good in some ways. It was more that she couldn't shake
the feeling he'd been distracted even in the middle of it.
Worse still, that she had been too.

Lyra wanted a re-enactment, to properly assess how she

felt about him. Then she could decide whether to "fish or cut bait", as Mick would phrase it.

She took extra care getting ready and was pleased that Miles noticed her as soon as she walked in the door and joined the girls at their usual barrel.

"Hey." He pecked Lyra lightly on the cheek. "How are you ladies? Annie? Mara?"

"It's Amy and Marley," Lyra corrected him.

"Right." He sounded as though he hadn't heard. "I'll bring your drinks over."

Lyra smiled. He might not remember her friends' names, but he remembered their drinks. That was something.

"How's The Pie-ganic?" Marley asked, adjusting the oversized pussy-bow on her bright yellow blouse. It appeared to be made of a curtain fabric, and she'd teamed it with orange track pants.

"It's okay," Lyra replied. "We're fighting off Alex's lamb with a vegetable pie."

"Oh, that's a cool idea." Amy's blue eyes twinkled in delight. "How come you guys never did anything vegetarian before?"

Lyra shrugged. "Actually, we hadn't thought of it. And we hadn't thought about playing music or having the tables outside either."

"Sounds like this friendly competition has been good for giving you new ideas," Marley said.

Lyra paused for a second. "I hadn't looked at it that way. But you're probably right. I was really worried at first that him showing up meant we were going to end up in another situation like the one in the city."

Amy and Marley winced, remembering that horrible time in Lyra and Silas's lives.

"Are there any signs that he's like that?" Amy asked.

Lyra considered, then shook her head. "Not really. He

praises our truck to other people, and comes over to congratulate us if we've had a good day. He actually doesn't seem that bothered one way or another."

"Why's he even doing it then?" Marley asked.

"I don't know," Lyra admitted. "He came on really strong in the beginning, with that awful sandwich board and then the lamb. But then…" she shrugged. "Nothing else happened except Silas and I picked up our game a bit."

"I think it's always like that, isn't it," Amy observed. "It's really nice having someone challenge you a little and help you lift your game. There's a new woman at work who does the most amazing stuff with patterns." Amy looked wistful. Her office was in Lilac Bay - about a fifteen minute walk from Lyra's truck, although she rarely had time to come visit. "She somehow clashes patterns and the effect is just amazing."

"Maybe she can do something for Silas and I," Lyra said, thinking of the sad, mismatched state of their apartment.

Amy looked stung. "You've never asked me to do anything like that for you."

"Oh! I would never make you do that. Wouldn't it be hard to tell us what you really thought? I mean, since we're such good friends and all?"

"Lyra," Marley said, suddenly deathly serious. "Your friends are supposed to be the ones who can tell you what they really think! That's the whole point of friendship!"

Lyra felt chastened and upset that she'd hurt Amy. She looked around anxiously for their drinks, but Miles was well over the other side of the bar, engaged in deep conversation with one of his female colleagues.

"Sorry," Lyra said awkwardly. "Amy, I would absolutely love for you to do something with our apartment. I know Silas would too. We just can't afford any advice. I was just kidding when I said your colleague could help."

"You think I'd charge you?" Amy frowned.

"Yes! As you should. No one should be giving their services away for free."

"So if I asked you to sing at my grandfather's funeral-"

"What's wrong with Percy?" Marley asked, horrified.

"At my grandfather's *hypothetical* funeral." Amy put a reassuring hand on Marley's arm. "You'd charge me?"

"Of course not."

"I rest my case." Amy slapped the barrel.

At that moment, Miles finally turned up and Lyra couldn't have been more grateful.

"A whiskey lemonade for you," he said, setting the glass down in front of her. "A cherry daiquiri for you my lady," he continued, putting the cocktail in front of a bemused Marley. "And your favourite, a tequila sunrise." He presented Amy the glass with a flourish.

There was an awkward silence.

"These aren't our drinks," Marley said bluntly. Lyra flushed. Miles was stunned into silence for a second.

"It's absolutely fine," Lyra said quickly. "Change is as good as a holiday."

She took a sip of her whiskey lemonade, which until that moment she had not known was a thing, and then tried to stop her face from spasming. Marley stirred her daiquiri sceptically.

"So," Amy said brightly to Miles, not even laying a hand on her cocktail. "Who's the entertainment tonight?"

"Oh, this local chick, wait till you hear her." Miles was instantly animated. "She just does amazing stuff with sound. It's really avant-garde."

"You don't have many male singers in here, do you?" Marley asked.

Miles shrugged. "We really like to push local female talent. It's kind of our thing."

"*Your* thing," Marley said. "Don't you pick all the acts?"

He nodded and turned to Lyra, obviously awkward with the turn of the conversation. "Speaking of which, Lyra, I still haven't heard from your manager."

Marley coughed. Lyra looked down at her drink. "Oh, she'll call," Lyra said vaguely. "We've been a little busy, but I'll get her onto it this week. Promise."

"Good," he said. "Gotta dash, I'll be back later."

He pecked her lightly on the cheek again. But not, Lyra noticed, before glancing around to see who could see. It was obvious he couldn't get away from the table fast enough.

"Thanks, Marley," Lyra said when he was gone, trying to keep her voice calm.

"For what?" She blinked.

"For being so rude that you chased him away."

"How on earth was she rude?" Amy asked, and Lyra instantly felt her face flame. Amy had never taken Marley's side over hers before. There hadn't been many occasions that called for side-taking, but Lyra had always assumed that Amy would be in her corner no matter what. Lyra was so hurt she was speechless for a moment.

"Well, she didn't need to point it out about the drinks," she said finally.

"But if he can't remember, he should ask." Amy said, practically. "What even is this?" She shoved her tequila sunrise away in horror.

"It's a drink. What's your problem, Amy?"

"I don't have one, but I think you might. That guy is not good enough for you, Lyra. You're being ridiculous about him. You should see yourself, bending over backwards. It's embarrassing. What is happening to you?"

A silence fell and Lyra's heart thumped, colour staining her cheeks. She didn't trust herself to speak for a moment.

"It was nice that he brought us drinks at all," she said

finally. "We can all drink something different for once, especially since they're on the house."

"He left a bill for them." Marley held it up triumphantly. Lyra sighed.

Just then, a petite brunette with bombshell proportions and baby-doll eyes walked in, clutching a violin case. Lyra watched as all heads, including Miles's, turned towards her.

"Oh look," Amy said sarcastically. "It's Avant Garde."

Lyra felt like Amy was deliberately trying to shame her. The whole evening was going nothing like she'd planned. Amy was in a strange, snippy mood. Marley was pointing out every tiny little thing. And Miles was…well, she had no idea.

"I think I'm going to go home." She felt childish and sensitive as she said it, but she wasn't completely in control of her emotions. "I'll pay for this round since he messed it up so badly."

She fished for her wallet, hoping one of them would stop her. Instead, she saw them share a slightly exasperated look that made her face burn.

"Lyra, I think you've blown this out of proportion," Amy said.

"You're in a weird mood," Marley added.

"Well, then it won't matter if I just get out of your way then, will it?" she said, fighting tears. She tossed money on the table, grabbed her jacket and headed for the door.

Miles cut her off just as I reached it.

"Hey, hey, hey." He grabbed her arm. "Where are you off to?"

"I'm just a bit tired." She froze so he wouldn't take his hand off her.

"I'll walk you out." Lyra turned to see whether the girls were looking after her. They were completely absorbed in their own conversation.

Miles and Lyra stood in the cool air for a moment. He

looked her up and down, an appraising smirk on his face. Lyra had nothing to say, once again.

Suddenly, he pulled her close and kissed her. It was gentle and slow, and this time it left her tingling when he finally pulled away.

She leaned into him, feeling emboldened. "Hey," she said, smelling his shirt and resting her whole torso against his. The affection felt good.

"Hey," he said, huskily. He leaned in for another kiss, but Lyra wanted to say something. She pulled back out of his reach and he grinned, thinking she was teasing him.

"The girls who sing here..." she began hesitantly.

Instantly his face clouded over. "What about them?" He took a step back. She tried to draw him to her, but he stood firm. Lyra felt silly and school-girlish.

"They're always so...attractive."

That seemed to set something off in him and he broke away from her completely. "Listen, Lyra." His face was stony. "I really hate possessiveness. Like, really hate it. I can't be monitored like this."

"I'm not monitoring you," she said defensively, but he was shaking his head. "I don't even know what we are, so why would I monitor you?"

"Oh, the old 'what are we' question."

"No-"

"You're really cool and everything, but I'm not looking for a girlfriend and I'm definitely not looking to be nagged."

"I wasn't -"

He cut her off by lunging towards her and kissing her again, this time passionately. She was left breathless at the end of it.

"That's what it's like if you're with me." He stood back to study her reaction. She supposed she looked flushed and off-centred, since that's how she felt. "But I'm really not into this ball and chain business. You handle yourself, you know that work is work and that I need to get involved with the acts, and you give me that space. That's how it is. Or..." he held his palms up and shrugged, "or it just isn't."

And with that, he turned and headed back inside, leaving Lyra standing there - unsure what she was feeling and what had just happened. Miles had kissed her three times exactly, and she hadn't felt prepared for any one of them.

She pulled on her jacket and started to walk slowly home, her thoughts in turmoil. Was that the kind of thing she wanted, what Miles seemed to be offering? Something casual?

Surely, she should be strong enough within herself to accept that there were beautiful women all around the world, on every single corner, and that he was going to come into contact with them. Maybe it would teach her to overcome any petty jealousies, to be a stronger person. Still, something wasn't sitting right.

As she walked home along brightly lit streets, her jacket zipped tight against the evening chill, she found herself thinking again of Alex, and Alison. She tried to remember exactly what Alison had told her that day she'd been crying at the hospital. She remembered only that Alison had said she'd cheated, and had moved out. It had happened at around the same time Alex had appeared to claim the spot beside them on the promenade.

Lyra's heart hurt for Alex. He didn't deserve to be cheated on, but Alison was a good person and had seemed devastated and confused by her own actions. Lyra thought about what Mick had said, about his own wife cheating on him. *There's always two sides to the story.* Lyra wondered what Alex's side was. It was a story she'd be interested in hearing, if he ever spoke to her again. That, and what on earth he was doing with a lamb.

Her mind lost in these thoughts, she only looked up when she neared the last block before home - the restaurant quarter. She pulled her phone from her jacket pocket to check whether the girls, or Miles, had messaged. They hadn't. She lowered the phone and stared absently into the restaurant she was standing in front of for a moment.

As she focused her eyes, shock ran through her. Alex was dining in a window seat in the corner, sitting across from a beautiful, dark-haired woman who gazed at him with love in her eyes. Candles glowed on their table, bathing them in warm light, and they seemed to be having a great time. His face lit up as she said something to him, and they both laughed like old and intimate lovers. After a moment, he raised a fork to his mouth and Lyra did a double-take. He was eating a steak. A *steak.*

She was instantly enraged. What kind of game was he playing, running a truck called *Meat is Murder* and posting horrific pictures of animals, all the while eating meat himself? Maybe he was just like the people from the city after all. Maybe he even knew them. It didn't matter that he appeared not to be trying too hard to ruin their business, or that he was complimentary in person. That was the kind of thing someone *would* do if they were trying to build up trust before they stuck the knife in!

Lyra headed to the restaurant door, fuelled by anger and the annoyance of all the evening's events.

Thankfully, she mastered herself before barging in. She had a better idea. And it would fight fire with fire if Alex tried to play tricks again.

As soon as she got home, she stormed into Silas' room with her phone thrust out in front of her.

"What am I looking at here?" Silas squinted at the screen and shrugged.

"Zoom in on that couple dining."

"What? No, why?" Silas shied away from the phone.

"Just do it!"

He picked the phone delicately out of her hands and pinched the photo to zoom in. His eyes bulged and he burst out laughing.

"Why are you laughing?"

"He's not really vegan at all!"

"No! He isn't!" She took the phone back, irritated that Silas wasn't upset.

"So it's all an act," Silas said. "That's hilarious."

"How on *earth* is it hilarious?"

"Because it's a good angle to play. Bravo to him. Anyway, he's never truly hurt our business. Our numbers are rising, pretty steadily. If anything, more people come out now, from even further away. It looks like there are options for them, even though most of them come to us."

Nothing about the night had gone the way she'd planned. She wanted to hit reset on the whole day and try again. She wouldn't call the girls, she wouldn't say anything to Miles about the other singers, and she wouldn't know a thing about Alex and his beautiful date.

"Well, I find it extremely odd. And I'm going to keep this up my sleeve to put on a sandwich board beside his truck."

Silas frowned. "Don't be ridiculous."

"I'm not saying I'll do it, but if he brings out that other sandwich board, we can retaliate. His customers have a right to know about this."

"Do they? Why are you upset?"

"Why aren't you?"

Silas took a step back and surveyed her, a slow grin spreading across his face. "You like him! That's why you're

97

annoyed at this photo. It's got nothing to do with his *ethics*. You're upset he's on a date."

She was silent. "It might not even be a date, so why would I care?"

"Oh, Lyra." He palmed his forehead.

"You're wrong! I have something going on with Miles, I'm not the least bit interested."

"You can tell yourself that all you want." Silas raised his eyebrows and didn't finish the sentence.

"I hate everyone!" She snatched her phone from Silas and stormed to her room, slamming the door for good measure.

Once she was alone, she started to cry. She sat on her bed, staring at a picture of her mother cradling her as a baby. Then she pulled it to her chest, hugging it and wishing her mother was still here. Mothers could always comfort their children, no matter which mood they were in, or how unreasonable they were being.

Deep down, Lyra knew that was unlikely to be true, but it was a fantasy she had clung to since they'd lost her. The anniversary of her death was drawing near. Winter would always be connected with a sense of loss for Lyra. Even if she remembered very few details about the months before her mother's death, she always remembered that the days had been getting colder and shorter before they lost her. So that it had felt like all the light and warmth in the world were disappearing at once.

Alex's cardigan was draped over the foot of her bed and she sat up to pull it on. She flopped onto her back, clutching the picture in one hand and dashing away tears with the other. Lyra felt like she was on an emotional rollercoaster, and there was one person - alive - who could help her when she felt like this. She texted Mick to see if he was well enough to rehearse that weekend.

CHAPTER SEVENTEEN

Lyra carefully examined Mick's face when he opened the front door. The stitch was already out and he'd have an extra small scar, but that seemed to be it.

"These from your brother?" Mick asked, as Lyra held out more pies.

"Uh...from both of us," she said finally. She hadn't mentioned the pies to Silas at all. Mick's face dropped a little. "Haven't you spoken to him?" Lyra asked, pained.

Mick shook his head. "We'll chat soon enough, don't you worry."

He turned to take the pies to the fridge and Lyra sensed the conversation was over. They headed for the garage to rehearse.

Ten minutes later, Mick lifted his fingers from the keyboard to stop the music.

"What's going on?" Lyra asked. "Why did you stop? We're just getting started."

"The line is 'down to the water we go'."

"What did I say?"

"Drowned in the water like roe.... for the third time."

"I'm sorry, Mick." She slumped at the microphone. They kept it turned off when they rehearsed, but Lyra liked it in front of her. There had been times in the early days of getting on stage where she hadn't really known what to do with it, and had either hugged it too closely or shied away from it. Neither were great for sound. She wanted to keep working on being more natural with it.

"You want to talk about what's really going on?" Mick asked gently.

She stepped away from the mic and paced Mick's garage. They had two small gigs coming up and she couldn't get her head in the game.

"Not really," she said. But that was a lie. She hadn't heard from the girls and wasn't quite sure how to reach out to them to bridge the gap. Silas was still laughing at her, which was driving her crazy. She and Miles hadn't spoken or exchanged messages since the night at the Whistle Stop, and she didn't know what to do about having caught Alex out as a liar.

Her head was in complete turmoil. Where would she even start explaining it to Mick? And the poor man had enough of his own issues. Why did she have to burden him with hers?

Mick was watching her with his head cocked to one side. As always, she had the feeling he could see right through her. Sure enough, he gestured to the table and chairs.

"Let's have a beer and talk about it."

She sighed heavily and gave up, nodding. It was what she had wanted all along.

He pulled two beers from the garage fridge. They cracked them and sat at the small table, but didn't open the roller door. The day was quite cool and they both wore jumpers.

"It's about a dumb guy," she said finally, when they'd been sitting there a few moments in silence. "Or...maybe two. And it's about my girlfriends. Actually...it's mostly about my girl-friends. And it's about Mum."

"Ah." Mick nodded, looking down. "Well, let's start with the easy thing. The guys."

"There's a guy I met at the Whistle Stop. I'm attracted to him, but we really haven't had a chance to get to know one another that well. Sometimes he seems to like me, and then..."

Mick let her sit there in silence for a moment, before prompting.

"He's inconsistent?" She nodded. "I'm not the best at giving advice, but I've been in similar situations and I'll pass on the thing that helped me the most." She swigged her beer and looked at him expectantly. "Pay attention to how you feel around him. *You*. Not how he's treating you, not what he's saying. How comfortable you feel. How noticed you feel. How heard you feel. And how much like *you* you feel."

She nodded slowly, knowing he was right. Being around Miles made her feel a little invisible and competitive. She knew those were bad signs.

"If he got to know me, *really* got to know me -"

"Decision is yours," Mick said, cutting her off. "But life's pretty short - especially if the universe keeps trying to take it from you. You've got to move on, either with or without this guy."

She let the words sink in. "You're right."

"I know. Now, what about the other guy?"

That was more difficult. "He works in the food truck next to us. He's...he's very good-looking." An image of Alex's tall frame, his thick hair and those grey eyes flashed into her mind. She swallowed it down with a swig of beer. "He came to watch us play that night at Rusty's-" Mick winced, "And he came to the hospital afterwards. But, remember that time Alison the nurse was crying and I said she'd cheated on someone?" He nodded. "It was him. She'd cheated on him.

And he's also…hard to figure out, I guess. His food truck is vegan, but I saw him in a steak restaurant with a beautiful woman. He brings a lamb to the truck, I guess to discourage people from our food, but he doesn't really seem competitive in any other way."

"And?" Mick prompted.

"And what?"

"How do you feel when you're around him?"

She thought for a moment. Definitely calmer than when she was with Miles, that was for sure. And more certain about herself. Maybe because Alex told her he thought she was a good singer, or maybe because he'd made an effort to see that part of her life, which was more than Miles had done. Miles hadn't even offered to let her gig at the Whistle Stop, even though he was quite happy to grab her for random kisses when no one was around. She also didn't get tongue-tied around Alex, the way she did around Miles. Even though she definitely found Alex more attractive.

"I feel…like myself."

Mick nodded once. "I think we've answered that question."

"But I don't even know if he likes me. I thought he did, but I saw him on a date."

"I don't know if he was on a date or not, but I can tell you you're making a lot of assumptions about him. About why he brought this goat along-"

"Sheep." Lyra grinned.

"About who he's dining with. It's simpler if you just clear these things up. Do you reckon he likes you?"

Lyra thought about it. There were occasional signs that he did. Or at least there had been until the night they saw Alison. Lyra also realised Alex still thought she was in a relationship. If his girlfriend had cheated on him, it made sense he would hold himself back from her if he thought she was attached.

Lyra needed to clear that up before anything else could happen. But what was the point if he really had been on a date? He and the woman he'd been with had looked very cosy and loved-up. What else would they be doing, if not dating? Just days earlier though, she could have sworn he was showing signs of interest.

Mick could see she was working through things. "So, what's happening with your girlfriends?"

Lyra sighed and told him briefly about the evening. It had felt like both girls had turned against her. Mick listened in complete silence until she finished.

"Well, you're just embarrassed," he said finally.

"Yes, that's the whole point. They made me feel stupid."

Mick shook his head. "Only one person can make you feel stupid." He pointed to her. "Sounds like they maybe could have been a bit more considerate of your mood, but there's only one question now."

She waited, but he didn't share. "And what's that?"

"Are you going to wait for them to reach out to you, or swallow your pride and reach out to them? Friendships are precious. Never take them for granted." Lyra nodded. "I've known those girls almost as long as you have," he continued. "Neither of them would hurt a hair on your head deliberately. Everyone has strange moods, Lyra. People are inconsistent, it's what humans are all about. You can't predict how someone will act every single day. You can just decide whether you keep choosing them. If the bad times outweigh the good, it's time to stop choosing them. But that isn't the case here, is it?"

She hesitated before shaking her head. "I'll think about it. They also shouldn't take me for granted, right? I just want everything to be normal again. It's the only way I'll stop this horrible feeling, I guess."

He nodded and took another swig before pointing his beer at her. "Also, it's the only way we're going to make any money from this band."

CHAPTER EIGHTEEN

The following Monday evening, Lyra and Silas were enjoying their weekly ritual of reading books together in silence in the living room. Silas always poured himself a tumbler of whiskey, while Lyra nursed a tea.

They sat in the mis-matched overstuffed armchairs they'd found at a flea market - his corduroy, hers leather, shiny from age and use. There was a polished tree stump between them that they used as a table for the drinks. It was one of Lyra's favourite times of the week, and tonight it felt extra cosy as she was wrapped in Alex's cardigan. It was quickly becoming a treasured part of her wardrobe, even though she knew she had to give it back. She hadn't found time to wash it yet, but would do it on the weekend and then bring it into the truck.

They usually had a no-phone policy for Monday reading nights, but Lyra had begged for an exception since the birth of Margot.

Her phone rang and she answered the call on the third

ring - just before Silas lost it - with a professional but non-committal "Hello?"

"Is this Margot?" asked a male voice. It sounded vaguely familiar to Lyra, but the caller was standing outside on a busy street, so the connection wasn't great.

She coughed and sat up straighter, never quite able to seamlessly shift between her two personas. "Yes. This is she." Silas sipped his whiskey, raising his eyebrows and waggling his head while holding up his pinkie finger, as if to mock Margot's airs and graces. Lyra frowned at him.

"I'm interested in booking your clients for a wedding," the voice went on.

"Which client, please?" Lyra rustled some pages in her book to make it sound as though she was thumbing through a diary. Silas returned to his book, shaking his head in amusement.

"Uh, she's called Lyra. And the guy who comes with her who plays the keyboard."

"Mick. Yes. Right. I need the date and location of the nuptials, please."

"Yes, of course." He sounded a little nervous. "It's actually a bit short notice. They're getting married in four weeks."

"A winter wedding. How lovely." Margot was slightly miffed on behalf of her clients. Silas lowered his book to look at her again. "Can you tell me about the venue?"

"I just got put in charge of music as someone else fell ill and this detail wasn't sorted out, apparently. It's at a surf club on the Central Coast."

"Number of guests?"

"I think about...fifty? But it's an enthusiastic group," the man added. "And a lot of them are social media-savvy, so they can help amplify the presence."

Margot paused. She liked that. Then she calmly stated the fee, which he immediately accepted.

"So they're available?" He sounded very pleased. "I've seen them live and they're great."

"They're available, that's correct. I'll need to confirm back with them of course. In the meantime, I'll send through the booking form and the bank account for the deposit. The deposit needs to be paid in the next two weeks. It's non-refundable and there's a thirty percent cancellation fee." Margot was making this up as she went along. Lyra loved her!

"That's great!" the caller said enthusiastically.

Margot took down a number, and an email address that the caller seemed slightly embarrassed to relay. "Flight club, all one word?" Margot repeated.

"Yeah, I've been meaning to change it." He cleared his throat. "The couple are called Rosie and Matt Linbury, and I'm Alex."

Lyra froze. "Okay, thank you for reaching out. I have another call coming through so…" Margot hung up.

Silas was still shaking his head. "Margot is kind of a b-"

"You wouldn't say that if she was a man!" Lyra shouted before he could finish, and threw a cushion at his head. He ducked and laughed. "Si, that guy was called Alex."

"And?" He frowned. "Are we doing Monday reading night or not? Why's your face red?"

She looked at him, eyes wide. "I'm pretty sure that was *Alex* Alex."

CHAPTER NINETEEN

They were at work a couple of days later when Lyra asked, "You okay if I take a little walk?"

Silas was busy texting someone and nodded distractedly.

She took off her apron and walked down to the water line. The sky was overcast and, though there was no rain, the bay was choppy and grey. Small gusts of wind worked up little waves that dashed against the low bank. She stayed there for a long moment, breathing in the salt mist and watching ferries criss-cross the harbour beyond. Being by the water always took the edge off her tension.

She wandered over to Murgatroyd and Alex, who was feeding him. The lunchtime rush was over, and it seemed Alex might stay longer. He'd been packing up and making a quick getaway most days. Lyra imagined he wanted to spend more time with the beautiful woman from the restaurant.

"Hey, Lyra." Alex smiled and straightened up. "How's Mick? I've been meaning to ask."

She flapped her hand. "Nothing can keep him down, he's fine. We're already back to rehearsing."

He smiled. "I'm glad to hear it. He seems like the type to spring back."

"You have no idea."

"Listen." He scuffed the toe of his sneaker on the ground and stuffed his hands into his jeans pockets. "I've wanted to talk to you about that night at the hospital…"

"I'll bring the cardigan back soon, I promise. I just have to wash it."

"Huh? Oh." He shook his head. "Take as long as you need. I would like it back at some stage, my favourite aunt knitted it for me. But no rush." She nodded. "So…Alison," he continued. "I take it you two know each other?"

"Yeah, a bit. We're not close. I did figure out…" She trailed off, and Alex nodded.

"I thought so. Allie's a good woman. It wasn't meant to be between us, looking back I can see that now. Don't think badly of her…if you were going to."

Lyra felt her heart rate increase. He was defending her honour. So many times she'd heard men talk about their *crazy ex-girlfriends.* Here was Alex making sure she knew that the woman who had cheated on him wasn't bad. Lyra felt an almost overwhelming urge to hug him. Then she remembered his date, and the steak. He'd definitely bounced back quickly from everything, into the arms of another woman.

"Ernie seemed really into Silas," Alex said, obviously trying to keep the conversation going.

"Everyone's really into Silas," Lyra said wryly. "You have no idea what it's like growing up with a beautiful sibling."

She hadn't meant to sound self-pitying; it was meant to come off lightly. She felt lightly about it. Silas was beautiful and that was a plain and simple fact. She smiled to show she hadn't meant it in a bitter way.

Alex seemed to be working up to say something and stared briefly out over the choppy water. Just as his mouth opened, Lyra cut him off - not wanting any words of hollow consolation.

"How committed are you to being vegan exactly?" As she heard the words come out of her mouth, she knew this wasn't going to go well. Her tone was off, there were too many emotions swirling through her.

Alex looked quizzical, thrown by the turn of conversation. "What?"

"I mean, to be running a food truck called Meat is Murder, and to have gone to the trouble of bringing Murgatroyd here and all."

He looked slightly uncomfortable. "I...it's important to me, you could say."

"When did you make that choice?"

Alex looked away, patted Murgatroyd. "Oh, a while ago, I guess," he said vaguely.

"Really? So, even when you're not here pushing your agenda on our customers - "

"I don't *push* anything." He sounded stung.

"Even when you're not doing that, you're vegan? Anything else would be hypocritical, wouldn't it?"

Alex squinted at her, shoving his hands deep into his jean pockets again. The afternoon light caught his eyes and hair, which looked freshly cut. Lyra realised it must have been a home job, because there was a little part just above his ear that was longer than the rest. For some reason, this detail made her heart swell. Until the thought struck her that maybe his girlfriend had cut it. She shook the thoughts out of her head in annoyance.

"What's going on, Lyra?"

She shrugged. "I'm just asking questions."

"Doesn't sound like it..." He cocked his head at her. Murgatroyd bleated and Alex stroked the lamb's head absently.

"Well imagine I'd been out the other evening and walked past a restaurant." She saw him swallow but he remained otherwise poker-faced, his eyes trained intensely on hers. She raised an eyebrow. "And imagine that I happened to look inside. What do you think I saw?"

Alex shrugged. "People eating?"

"Yes. That's exactly what I saw." He looked bemused. "And someone at the restaurant was eating a steak that looked so juicy and the person eating it looked so comfortable that I couldn't help...snap a little photo. One I think our customers have every right to see."

Instantly he caught her meaning. His eyes narrowed. "You were spying on me?"

"No! I walked past the restaurant and saw you and your date-"

"It wasn't a-" he began and then stopped himself, biting his lip.

"At first, I thought it couldn't have been you, because this person was eating *steak*. And after the performance you've put on here, with your sandwich boards and your Murgatroyd, I just didn't see how it could be." Alex's face had reddened as she was talking. She couldn't tell what he was thinking, although there were warning signs in his eyes that she was crossing some sort of line. Still, she pushed on. "What I'm thinking of doing," she said, "is blowing this picture up and putting it on a sandwich board. What do you think of that? I'd blur your girlfriend's face out of course-" she was on a roll and couldn't stop herself. The anger was coming from somewhere. She hated hearing it, but seemed powerless against it.

"She's not-"

"But I think your customers, people like that lady who comes past on her jogs, would be very interested to know that the owner of Meat is Murder is a murderer himself!"

She hadn't been able to stop her voice from rising, and a couple passing by stopped in their tracks to stare at them, probably trying to judge whether or not this was a situation that required intervention.

Alex was silent for a moment and Lyra could tell he was struggling with his emotions.

Finally he said in a low voice, "You have absolutely no idea what you're talking about. I don't appreciate being stalked."

"I wasn't stalk-"

"And I *don't* appreciate being called a liar. You can do whatever you want with your stupid photo, but you should try and get your facts straight before you go about destroying this business."

They stared at each other for a long moment. "You really have absolutely no idea, do you?" he said. He bit the inside of his cheek, as if he was struggling to stop himself from saying something, and then it burst out of him anyway. "How come I never see your boyfriend around here? Does he come visit you? Does he watch you sing?"

Lyra was stunned into silence. Why was he bringing that up? At least it was clear he *did* think she was in a relationship. But what did it matter, if he was in one too? Lyra shook her head slowly, all the wind gone out of her sails. She hadn't intended for things to get this heated with Alex.

"I'm not...I don't-" She shook her head to indicate there was no relationship, no boyfriend. Alex was watching her closely.

"Hey!" Silas suddenly shouted, glaring at Alex and Lyra.

"What?" she called back, turning to him.

"Stop *flirting* and come and help me here. We need to clean up!"

Lyra turned back and Alex was still watching her, his expression unreadable.

She drew a huge deep breath, mumbled "sorry" as inaudibly as she could and shuffled off back to Silas. In the reflection of the truck, she saw him staring after her.

CHAPTER TWENTY

The following week was one of the longest of Lyra's life. Silas often had to call her back to earth when she drifted off, phone in hand, trying to figure out a way to compose a message to Amy and Marley. Mick's advice had helped; she knew it needed to be her who extended an olive branch. She was just having trouble over-coming her natural stubbornness. It hurt, because she wanted so badly to talk things through with them.

Alex didn't turn up the day immediately following their argument. When he did come back, he kept to himself and smiled somewhat sadly at her every time they made eye contact. Lyra had even lingered out by the tables once or twice, taking so long to clean them that Silas got frustrated. She'd been hoping it would encourage Alex to come over. But it seemed he was just as reluctant to take the first step as she was.

To break the ice, she wanted to ask him whether he'd been the one who called Margot about the wedding. Except she couldn't find a credible way she'd have that information. Margot had never heard Alex's voice before.

Lyra went for long walks during her breaks, most often sitting in the Secret Garden, staring at the blank or scribbled-over pages in her song book, wondering when inspiration would strike. Surely her dry spell couldn't last much longer.

Miles texted twice during the week, both times at 3am. Both times she'd had her phone off and been fast asleep. She had not bothered to reply the following day.

Occasionally, in the privacy of a bench deep within the garden, she would find herself looking at the picture she'd taken of Alex and his date. He looked happy and relaxed and the woman sitting across from him was beautiful, her dark eyes sparkling and trained adoringly on his. It made sense.

Alex was very handsome, becoming more so to her every day.

❖

A lone figure walked up and down the Lilac Bay promenade. His hood was pulled down over most of his face, and he was hunched despite the unseasonable mildness of the day. He walked back and forth several times, feigning complete nonchalance.

Lyra recognised him as the short, skinny kid from the group of teenage boys who'd shrieked at Murgatroyd that day. The one who'd tried to stop them from upsetting the lamb. Now, it seemed he was trying to get up the courage to approach the pen. Lyra wondered whether Alex had noticed and watched the situation with interest.

After another brisk walk past their trucks, the teenage boy turned once more to cruise by. This time, it seemed he'd worked up enough nerve to approach Murgatroyd. Slowly, hesitantly, the boy inched closer to the pen, until Alex stepped out of his truck. The boy quickly veered off, pretending he hadn't intended to come near at all. But Alex called out to him gently and beckoned him closer.

The boy hesitated for a long moment, then cautiously approached. Alex held a warm bottle of Murgatroyd's formula out to him, and after a little coaxing, he took it. The lamb had spotted it and was leaping around joyously. He sprang over to the boy and began to suck greedily from the bottle, desperate to get the milk out as quickly as he could.

The boy stroked Murgatroyd's head, transfixed. A slow grin spread over his face as he eased into his role as feeder, looking like a natural. He and Alex started a conversation and kept talking until Murgatroyd's bottle was empty. They stood talking for a few moments longer as the lamb licked the boy's hand for any remaining drops, then ambled away. The whole scene had warmed Lyra's heart and made her feel a rush of tenderness towards Alex.

Frank came by at that moment, in a chatty mood. Silas seemed a little sullen, so Lyra made up for it by getting into a long conversation with Frank about the weather and the goings-on at the building where he worked in maintenance. It seemed like a soap opera there sometimes. With the haughty chefs from the nearby restaurant, maintenance workers having affairs with each other and the cleaning staff living a version of an upstairs-downstairs English period drama.

By the time Frank left with his usual pie order and a drink, the teenager had gone and Alex was back inside his van. The lunchtime rush started up and a longer than usual line reached back to the water. They sold out of four varieties of pies, and Silas kept a tally, as he always did, so he'd know how much of each to order from Jan for the following day.

Once the rush was over and they'd cleaned up the tables outside, Lyra stepped out to stretch her legs. She found herself drawn to Murgatroyd, wondering where he thought he was, what he thought was happening. She had never considered sheep or lambs as pets, hadn't really considered them at all, but it was clear Murgatroyd had some kind of bond with Alex. Alex was out there with him every moment he had free, caressing him, letting Murgatroyd jump all over him, bottle feeding him. Still, did the lamb have enough room to roam? Wasn't it at least a little cruel to keep him in a small pen?

Murgatroyd trotted to the edge of the pen to greet Lyra and, without thinking, she reached over and stroked his head.

"He's growing up fast," Alex said, surprising her a little so that she jerked and alarmed Murgatroyd. "Sorry, I didn't mean to scare you...I've just never seen you pay him any attention."

Lyra shrugged and kept her eyes on the lamb, finding it hard to look directly at Alex. He continued talking, gently and in a low voice - as though Lyra were the lamb and could be spooked. "He was orphaned, and I heard about him through a friend of mine who's a vet. They needed someone to care for him for a couple of weeks, give him his formula every couple of hours, keep him warm, get him his shots, give him outdoor time." She nodded to show she was listening. "He'll be ready to go back to his farm soon," Alex said, "But I'm going to miss him at home. He came along at a good time for me..." he trailed off and Lyra knew what he meant. Murgatroyd had come along after Alison had moved out.

"He sleeps with you?" Lyra asked, avoiding the Alison topic and looking up at him. Their eyes caught and she looked away again. There was a lot she wanted to say, but she didn't really know where to start.

"Well, not *with* me, but in the house, yes. It's completely impractical, but it's the only way to keep him warm enough.

Me and Murgs, just two bachelors living the life. Doesn't smell the greatest at my place right now, let me tell you."

Lyra couldn't help but chuckle, and her mind grabbed hold of the word "bachelors" and replayed it. Had he broken up with the woman from the restaurant? Or had they never been together?

"Look, I'm sorry about the whole photo thing," she said.

"Don't be," he said quickly. "I know you weren't stalking me and I shouldn't have accused you of it."

"Well, it *was* weird of me," she admitted. "Although I am still surprised that you eat meat, when you have…" she swept her arm around, meaning the food truck and the lamb. "Although it's a bit less surprising now I know why Murgatroyd is here."

"There's a lot I want to explain to you, Lyra," he said gently, and she felt her heart beat a little faster. She was aware of how closely they were standing. She could see the scar under his lip, and she concentrated on it, afraid to look into his eyes. *There's a lot I want to know,* she thought. But then Alex shoved his hands into his pockets again.

"I'm just - I'm not in the right place for…anything just now." There was a strange note in his voice.

Lyra couldn't help but bristle a little at his words. Was he saying that for her benefit, or for his? Did he think she needed to be warned off? She mentally scanned through her past actions, but she had done nothing that would indicate she wanted a relationship with him. *He* was the one who had turned up at her gig and at the hospital. The one who had asked about her boyfriend, more than once. The one who had likely booked her to sing at a wedding. She had snapped his picture and confronted him with it, but her motives for that had been purely business…as far as he knew. They stood there in silence for a moment, listening to the gentle lap of the small waves against the bank. She opened her mouth to say something but at that moment, Silas called out to her. His timing was impeccable, as always.

She nodded to Silas and looked back at Alex.

"I'm single," she said. It made her feel vulnerable, but she wanted Alex to know. "I have been this whole time. Silas…" she waved a hand. "But you don't need to worry about me trying to start anything. You didn't need to warn me off."

Alex frowned, then registered her meaning and looked surprised. He quickly shook his head and opened his mouth but before he could speak, she added, "It's good you were nice to that kid."

She turned to walk swiftly back to the truck. When Lyra looked back a moment later, Alex was looking out into the harbour, his posture downcast.

Her phone pinged with a message as she tied her apron back on. She saw Amy's picture in the preview and quickly swiped to read it. *Marley and I will be at WS tonight if you want to join us.*

CHAPTER TWENTY-ONE

Lyra was nervous walking into the Whistle Stop, hanging by the entrance and scanning for the girls. Rick was with them. He spotted her first and broke into a big smile, beckoning her over. Lyra liked Rick a lot. He was relaxed company, obviously completely smitten with Amy and, once the girls had broken past his shy exterior, they'd discovered he had a wicked sense of humour.

Lyra greeted Amy and Marley. To an outsider it might have seemed like a warm greeting, but Lyra could feel the thin wall of ice between the three of them - or more accurately, between the two of them and her. All she wanted from this evening was to somehow break it, preferably without too much damage to her ego.

They made stiff, polite conversation until their drinks kicked in and the ice started to thaw. Miles was nowhere to be seen, and Lyra felt relieved.

"I think I'm swearing off men altogether," she said, looking into her vodka soda.

"But there must be good ones out there," Rick said

encouragingly. "Well, Amy got the last one for now." He pointed two thumbs to himself. "But there'll be a round of divorces soon, and you can really clean up then."

"What about Alex?" Amy sipped her drink and eyed Lyra.

She shook her head. "First, his van is called Meat is Murder, but I caught him in a restaurant eating steak. Eating actual steak." It wasn't nearly the most important thing that she wanted to talk about where Alex was concerned, but everything else was too uncertain and uneasy to discuss.

"What?" Marley shrieked. "That's despicable!"

"I know. I actually confronted him about it."

"At the restaurant?" Amy asked.

Lyra squirmed. "No, actually, what I did was a bit worse. I took a photo through the window and then confronted him."

Amy raised her eyebrows but said nothing.

"Despicable!" Marley repeated.

"It's not that big of a deal, really." Lyra wished she hadn't brought it up. Marley would likely take hold of the topic and not let go.

"But he had nothing to say about it?" Amy asked.

Lyra shook her head. "But anyway, everything else is fine between us."

"Well," Amy said flatly. "He's a liar. So he's out."

"Amy, he was never in!" Lyra said, a little too defensively.

Rick was staring at Amy. "Wait a minute. We don't know what this guy lied about, or if he even lied at all."

Amy shrugged. "He runs a food truck called Meat is Murder, puts out militant vegan billboards and then eats steak in a restaurant? Sounds like a liar to me. At the very least a giant hypocrite."

"Sometimes lies protect people," Rick said.

"No." Amy shook her head vigorously. "There is never, ever a reason to lie."

Out of the corner of her eye, Lyra noticed Miles arrive at the bar to start his shift. She waited for her pulse to start racing, but it didn't.

"What about if he really likes Lyra, but he thought she'd only fall for a vegan?" Rick said.

"I work in a meat pie truck," Lyra pointed out. "He literally only knew me as the woman selling meat pies."

"Well, what about if he thought-"

Amy cut him off with a glare. "Are you trying to find reasons when a lie is acceptable? Because there aren't any!"

Lyra made a mental note to pull Rick aside later and explain something to him. Amy's father had quite literally gambled away their family home, telling lie upon lie to hide his habit from his family until long after it was too late. He'd ended up in prison and Amy had cut off all contact with him. Understandably, she was somewhat sensitive when it came to the topic of lies.

"I told my old flat-mates I have something called transmittable congenital herpes, so they'd stop eating my ice-cream," Marley said out of nowhere. They all burst out laughing.

"Hey, Lyra," Miles whispered, almost in her ear.

She jerked in surprise. "Miles." She smiled tightly. She wanted to concentrate on this bonding moment with her friends and hoped he wouldn't stay long.

"What did they say?" she asked Marley.

"They believed me," Marley shrugged, sipping her drink innocently.

"Amy? Verdict please," Lyra said. "Is this an acceptable use of white-lying?"

Amy squinted at them all in turn. "I'll allow it," she said finally, and Rick slapped the table jubilantly.

Lyra could sense Miles' agitation at being ignored. "Right, well, I better get to work," he said pointedly.

"Okay," Lyra said. "Oh wait!" He turned around with a knowing smile. "Anyone want a drink?" she asked, casting her eyes around the table questioningly. She registered the surprise on all three faces, then turned to see it on Miles as well.

He recovered well. He straightened up, placed a hand on her shoulder, massaging it lightly and looked at the others.

"One round of anything you guys want is on the house tonight," he said. "Friends of Lyra's are friends of mine."

"Shots," Amy said instantly and Rick laughed. "That will help us decide what to do about Alex and Lyra."

At the mention of a man's name, Miles' hand tightened on Lyra's shoulder and she flinched. "Shots it is! Thanks, Miles."

He looked confused and finally shrugged and smiled. "What the lady wants, the lady gets!" he said and walked off.

"He seemed really into you this time," Marley said.

"Only because she showed zero interest in him," Rick said.

Amy turned to look at him. He grinned. "What?"

"You're absolutely right," she said and leaned in to kiss him. "That's how some men work."

"No," he corrected. "That's how some *people* work."

Lyra and Marley exchanged a look as Rick and Amy flirted. Lyra was happy that things were feeling back to normal between her and Marley as well. She felt like an idiot for ever having let anything come between them, and for having been such a brat about her feelings.

"Are you going to run from me because I finally said you were my boyfriend?" Amy asked Rick.

"No, because you were my girlfriend from that very first night, whether you admitted it or not," he said, leaning into her.

Their voices had dropped and it was clear to Lyra and

Marley that nothing else existed for the pair. Just as their lips met, Lyra coughed loudly.

"I believe we were discussing *my* life right now?" She smiled to show she was joking. "So if the lovebirds wouldn't mind..."

Rick and Amy smiled and snuggled into each other. Lyra felt a pang of jealousy. Not over Rick, but because she realised she wanted something like what they had. Something honest, where both people were open about their feelings. It seemed hard to get that to happen, or at least for both people to be ready at the same time.

Miles appeared at the table again with a tray full of shots. "Thought I'd drop these by." He set the tray down and rested both his hands on Lyra's shoulders. "Two for each of you."

"Oh God, this will be the end of us," Lyra said.

"Zip it!" Amy said, grabbing two of the little glasses with her perfectly manicured hands and handing one to Rick. "Thanks, Miles," she said, sounding for all the world as though she was dismissing him.

He craned his head to look questioningly at Lyra. His face was very close to hers, but it was producing no effect on her. Her heart rate remained steady as a surgeon's hand.

"Thanks indeed," she said, and downed her shot before turning back to the group. Miles left.

Three hours later, all rifts between the girls had been firmly mended and reinforced with Lyra's teary request for forgiveness and Amy's equally teary request for hers. When Lyra apologised to her own reflection in the bathroom, she decided it was time to go home. More than time, her head was spinning from the shots and the vodkas she'd chased them down with. She hugged everyone tightly, told them soppily how much she loved them and stumbled to the door.

She didn't realise Miles had followed her. As she walked into the cool evening air, he called out to her. She turned.

"Why don't we go grab dinner one night next week? I'm not working on Tuesday."

Lyra shrugged and pulled her jacket tightly around herself. "Call me and I'll see if I'm free," she said, barely managing not to slur. "I can't give you an answer now, sorry."

CHAPTER TWENTY-TWO

When Lyra reached her flat, marginally more sober thanks to the bracing night air, she was surprised to see an unfamiliar jacket hanging on the rack by the door.

"Hello?" she called. Silence greeted her. "Si?"

"In my room," came the reply after a long delay. Lyra poured herself a glass of water from the kitchen tap and headed down the hall towards his room, kissing her Mum's portrait on the way.

"Who's visiting?" she asked as she approached. There was no response.

She swung open the door to Silas's room and could not have been more surprised if Murgatroyd had been there.

"Ernie?" she almost spat out some water. The two of them looked quite cosy, sitting on the bed beside one another in the low light of Silas's bedroom. It seemed they'd been watching a movie together. They weren't touching, but there was definitely an atmosphere in the room.

"Hi, Lyra," Ernie said brightly. Silas avoided her eye.

"Uh..." she was speechless for a moment, before pulling it

together. "It's great to see you!" she said, giving Ernie a hug. He looked back and forth between her and Silas and then stood up reluctantly.

"I'd better be going," he said.

"Oh, nonono. You don't need to do that," Lyra said quickly, mortified to have broken up whatever this was.

"It's late anyway." Silas yawned for effect and lay down on his bed. "Night, Ernie," he added, making no move to touch or reach out to Ernie, who hesitated a moment before heading for the bedroom door.

"Night," he replied, trying to sound casual.

"I'll walk you to the door" Lyra said, shooting Silas a meaningful look. Silas shrugged and pulled his blanket up around his chin.

At the door, she smiled encouragingly at Ernie. "He's got a tough exterior," she whispered, "but he's soft in the middle once you crack it. You'll see."

Ernie nodded, but looked as if he didn't dare believe it. Lyra hugged him goodnight before going back to Silas's room and practically pouncing on him.

"When did this start?" she demanded. Silas stubbornly rolled to face the wall and pulled the blanket halfway over his head. "Has anything happened between you?"

"Ew!"

Lyra noticed there was a framed drawing on Silas's nightstand signed by Ernie. Silas hadn't hidden it. Lyra smiled at the back of her brother's head.

"You're an idiot," she said fondly. He slowly turned back toward her.

"Make me a hot chocolate? The way Mum used to make them?"

Her eyes were instantly damp. Thinking about their mother's hot chocolate conjured blurry-edged memories of an all-encompassing warmth, safety and love that made

Lyra's heart ache. Losing her had created a hollowness that would never be filled. How different would their lives be if she had survived? How much more stable, how much more secure?

Lyra nodded, swallowing hard against the lump in her throat. She loved that her brother needed her, just as much as she needed him and they both still needed their mother. It made Lyra feel as though she was there with them for just a moment. She hoped that feeling would never stop.

"Of course I'll make you some hot chocolate." She stumbled into a wall. "I just might need some help."

They knew the recipe by heart, and the ritual of making the hot chocolate was sacred. They never took any shortcuts. Warm the milk - and it had to be proper, full-fat milk - in the medium-sized saucepan until it began to steam but did not boil. You had to be careful to make sure it didn't boil. Stir in the shaved chocolate - *because cocoa powder clumps,* Lyra could hear her saying - and the raw sugar, plus exactly two drops of vanilla essence per cup. Serve hot, add a marshmallow and sprinkle with a couple of grains of sea salt.

She and Silas sat opposite one another at the kitchen table, wrapping their hands around the chipped enamel mugs they kept only for hot chocolate. They'd found them once in a camping supply store and had been reminded immediately of the single pleasant family trip they could both remember. A week of camping in a place neither of them could recall the name of, but that had definitely involved a weird day trip to a small mining town and their mum getting very interested in panning for gold.

They were silent for a long moment, both lost in their memories.

"It's coming up soon," Lyra said finally, meaning the anniversary of her death. She felt completely sober now.

Silas nodded slowly. "Ly…" She raised her eyebrows expectantly and sipped. "You know she wasn't perfect, right?"

She set her hot chocolate down. "What do you mean?"

"You were only seven. You can't remember it all."

"Remember what all? All I remember is love."

"Yes," he nodded. "That was all I remembered, too."

"But?"

He was silent. Eventually he shook his head. "I just don't think we do her any favours to remember her as this perfect angel when she was a real person. That makes her less than she was."

Lyra pondered this as she sipped her hot chocolate. She'd thrown Alex's cardigan on, having never found the time to wash and return it. His smell was fading from it, but there were still moments when she caught a note of it. That happened now and she pulled the cardigan tighter around her.

"Did Mum do something in particular that you're talking about?"

Silas shook his head. "I just…I know you were only small. Her being gone and everything that followed, it might have made you remember things through rose-coloured glasses."

"I don't *need* rose-coloured glasses, because she was perfect. There are no memories I have that don't involve feeling safe and loved."

"You're right, we definitely had that. She was definitely safety and love. For us."

"So then what are you talking about?" She took another sip and closed her eyes to savour the taste. Drinking the hot chocolate was like taking a portal to the past, only whenever she tried to bring her mother's face to mind, it was getting harder and harder. It was cruel that time made everything fade this way.

"I'm not really talking about anything," Silas said finally. "I just want you to remember that she was a real person, and that real people make mistakes."

CHAPTER TWENTY-THREE

The morning of the wedding gig, Lyra woke up with butterflies in her stomach. She sprang out of bed, walked past Silas's closed door, and made as much noise as possible in the kitchen while preparing the coffee.

She found herself thinking of Alex. They'd started to develop something like a friendship, taking short breaks together at slow times of the day and exploring the Secret Garden. She loved showing him the hidden sculptures and interesting plants she'd discovered. Alex seemed glad of the distraction, since Murgatroyd had been returned to the farm, where he was apparently thriving.

Would she see Alex today? She tried to picture him in a suit, and felt her pulse pick up...

Twenty minutes later, Silas stumbled in, looking groggy. He raised his eyebrows at her.

"Did you want something?"

"I made pancakes," she said brightly, flipping the last one and bringing the heaped plate over to the dining table.

Silas took a seat, sighing. "Syrup," he commanded, putting his head in his hands. "And coffee. Much, much coffee."

Silas slowly came to life over the pancakes and coffee and Lyra was grateful. It felt as though it was going to be a long day waiting for the afternoon to arrive.

"How are you getting to the wedding?" Silas asked, scooping a slice of pancake through the pool of syrup on his plate. "Margot driving?"

"Actually, they're sending a car for us." She raised an eyebrow, giving him a fake haughty look.

"They are not," Silas said in flat disbelief.

"Well, okay. It's not so much a car as a minibus. And it's not so much for us as one for guests. It was already picking up some of the guests and a few of them live near here. So. But it's like a car!"

Silas raised an eyebrow. "It's practically a red carpet to a stretch limo."

After clearing up breakfast, they went through some accounting for The Pie-ganic. Sometimes Lyra couldn't believe they made such a good living from it. It often felt like too much fun to be lucrative.

"When you get famous, I have no idea what I'm going to do," Silas said.

"Oh, stop it," she said, batting his arm.

"I mean it. I can feel it in my bones. It's going to happen for you. Sooner or later." He smiled crookedly at her, one of the most emotional expressions in his range. "The thing is, I hate people," he said. "You're the nice one, and I don't want to work with anyone else."

"Silas," she said, laying a hand on his arm. "I haven't written an original song in months, we're only getting gigs because I lied about having a manager, and my keyboard player has been on death's door more times than I can count. I'm not going anywhere soon, don't you worry."

❖

Lyra took extra care with her outfit, trying to find an ensemble that would keep her warm enough for the evening, but not leave her sweating on-stage in what was turning out to be a magnificently mild winter's day.

"Wow," Silas said, appearing behind her in the bathroom mirror. "You look amazing. Wish I could go with you."

"I'll try and get you a catering gig for the next one." She saw Silas glance slightly nervously at his watch and spun to look at him.

"Ernie's coming over, isn't he?"

"So what?"

"You know he really likes you. Don't play with him," she warned.

"I'm not playing! I've told him where I stand and that I'm not interested. It's his problem if he isn't listening."

Lyra nodded, not wanting to get into a whole thing about it right before she left. The doorbell rang. "That'll be Mick! Come say hello?"

Silas shook his head. "I've got to clean my room. But don't let him get electrocuted or drowned or...I can't even think of another thing that could happen!"

"He'll be fine," she said, heading out of the bathroom. "Love you, Si!" She blew him a kiss over her shoulder and he blew one back.

She slipped into her shoes at the door and grabbed her handbag and a shawl. Mick looked dapper and was obviously as excited about the gig as she was. The lightning scar was showing, but he'd also somehow managed to work a bow tie into his outfit.

"You look smashing, young lady!" He leaned forward to peck her cheek as she stepped out. She noticed that he looked past her into the flat a little anxiously. "Your brother home?"

"Uh, yeah, he's getting ready for a visitor," she said, shutting the door. "You scrub up alright yourself!"

"You ready to break a leg out there?" he asked, as he held his elbow out to walk her to the curb and wait for the bus.

"Mick!" she slapped his shoulder. "You're not allowed to joke about things like that!"

The minivan was almost full when she and Mick got in and sat beside one another. The driver had helped Mick stow their equipment. Their fellow passengers were a blend of young and old, mostly conservatively dressed and Lyra mentally ran through the song list they had prepared, trying to guess what would get a crowd like this onto the dance floor.

Mick was silent beside her, lost either in his own thoughts or the ridiculously-sized broadsheet newspaper he'd inconveniently taken along for the trip. Lyra realised he was wearing his "lucky" socks and sighed. There was nothing lucky about the threadbare things - he'd been wearing them every single time something bad happened. But his logic was that since he hadn't actually died on those occasions, perhaps the socks had actually saved him from death. So he kept them glued to his feet.

There were two women sitting behind them on the bus. For a while, the chatter around Lyra was drowned out into a buzz, but eventually she found herself tuned into their conversation.

"But apparently he's been working on some food truck," one of them said. Her voice was quite high-pitched.

"On a food truck?" the other one asked, in a thick Cockney accent.

"And it's vegan!" added High-Pitched, and the two of

them burst out laughing. "You imagine him going without his steaks?"

"What's he doing that for then?" Cockney asked.

Lyra felt the hairs at the back of her neck stand up. Were they talking about Alex? She wanted everyone else on the bus to shut up so she could hear them talk.

"Apparently, he volunteered to man it for Jenny for a month or so when she got sick, but then he met someone he liked ...or something. I don't really get the whole story."

"What, like a customer?" asked Cockney, sounding surprised.

"Maybe? I don't know," said High-Pitched. "Anyway, he came to an agreement with Jenny that he'd keep doing it for a while. She's been in need of a break and he's still giving her all the money anyway."

"Well, that's daft. What's he living off, then?"

There was a silence, during which Lyra imagined High-Pitched shrugging. "He needed a distraction after all that business with the breakup."

She felt herself sweating, and struggled to open the tiny window beside her for some fresh air, before she made patches on her dress.

"Are you alright?" Mick asked, turning to her.

"Pssht!" She put a finger to her lips. He shook his head as if she was mad and went back to reading his enormous newspaper.

"Yeah, that was a sad business," Cockney said in a low voice.

Suddenly, a group toward the front of the bus started singing drinking songs, although it was barely afternoon, there were no drinks to be had, and everyone was stone cold sober. Lyra wanted to stand up and shush the lot of them, but High-Pitched and Cockney joined right in and it seemed that was all the story she was going to get.

They were surely talking about Alex. And they'd said *he met someone he liked.* She didn't dare think it could be her, but unless it was Silas or Jogging Lady - who managed to come past at least daily - there hadn't been anyone else. *Besides the woman in the restaurant,* she reminded herself. Her skin prickled and a nervous heat filled her body. She reminded herself Alex had booked her for this wedding. At least, she was fairly certain he had. That didn't necessarily mean anything though; he needed live music at short notice, he'd seen her play...she shouldn't read too much into it.

Annoyed at herself, she vowed to push all thoughts of Alex out of her head. They were there for a wedding, and they needed to make a good impression. Lots of business could come from word of mouth, but not if the singer forgot all the lyrics.

CHAPTER TWENTY-FOUR

The wedding venue was a surf house, built right into the sand with stunning floor-to-ceiling views of the ocean. The walkway down from the bus was scattered with white petals and guests first arrived at a huge green wall, where succulents spelled out "Rosie + Matt". It was made for social media and everyone stopped to pose in front of it - and be handed a glass of champagne - before heading inside. Lyra and Mick skipped the alcohol but posed for a photo.

"Put this on 'bundle' when I finally join," Mick said, pocketing his phone again.

"Bumble?" Lyra guessed. "The dating app? You'll have to crop me out of it!"

"Nah. Oldest trick in the book is to pretend other women are into you," he said, elbowing her.

"Why'd I put my arm around you?" she shook her head theatrically.

Once they were through the cool gold and cream tiled entryway, they were into a fairy world. The ocean shone a bright sapphire blue, the sand was pure shining gold. The sky was clear, with only the smallest of decorative fluffy clouds.

Everything inside was swaddled in rich cream tones, including the tables which were set with bouquets of wheat-coloured flowers atop round mirrors and small glittering tealights in glass jars. Paper lanterns beaded the ceiling in strings and the service staff were all dressed in cream. The effect was serene and beautiful.

The ceremony was to take place on the tiled balcony which was set with a canopy arch of dripping flowers. The balcony glass had been wiped to a gleaming crystal, so the view of the beach remained uninterrupted.

After the ceremony, guests would come inside to eat, hear speeches and hopefully dance. Dancing was always good. Dancing was what they wanted.

As Mick and Lyra surveyed the room appreciatively they were approached by a tall, sinewy woman in a black form-fitting dress who introduced herself as "Roberta, the wedding overseer". Her demeanour was friendly but firm and she directed them to set up in a corner of the room on the parquetry dance floor.

"Is Margot with you?" Roberta asked as Mick rolled their gear towards the designated area.

"Uh, no." He quickly flicked his eyes to Lyra.

"Good." Roberta ticked something off on her list. "We didn't order a meal for her so it's just as well."

"We get a meal?" Mick asked.

Roberta looked at him like he was simple, gave him a tight smile and curt nod, and stalked off.

"I think that's a yes," Lyra said, helping him with their gear. They giggled like school kids. Having never played a wedding, everything was new to them.

Matt, the groom, came over to introduce himself. He was tall, with close-clipped hair, and carried himself confidently, his shoulders squared. He seemed calm considering it was his wedding day, which gave Lyra a good feeling about the whole event. Maybe that was the benefit of hiring someone like Roberta. She could take care of any unpleasant business for you so you were free to enjoy your day.

"I've got a lot of army buddies coming," Matt said, instantly explaining the posture and hair. "Don't worry about them, they're a good crew."

"Also handy if a war breaks out," Lyra joked and Matt chuckled.

Mick and Lyra weren't worried about army types, just the kind of person who'd show up in a tracksuit, like the ones at Rusty's bar. Lyra thankfully didn't see any of those kinds.

She was on her knees fiddling with the base of the microphone stand when she heard Alex call her name. She froze and her heart quickened. So it *had* been him. She reminded herself to act surprised. Margot had taken that call, not her.

"Oh, hi!" she said a little awkwardly, getting to her feet. It was the first time she'd seen him in anything aside from jeans and a t-shirt. His grey-blue suit was perfectly tailored, the fabric almost the exact colour of his eyes. He wore a deep red pocket square and Lyra felt her face turning a similar colour.

Mick made himself busy as far from them as he possibly could. Lyra had already realised she was interested in Alex, but seeing him so handsome and polished, and being together somewhere other than Lilac Bay, set her heart on a wild course. It didn't help that he seemed just as affected by her.

"It's so great -" she said, at the same time as he said, "I'm so glad -"

They both stopped and laughed. "You go first," he said.

"It's great to see you here, that's all."

"Same." He smiled at her. "As soon as I heard you guys

play that night at Rusty's, I thought you'd be perfect. I called your manager right away."

Lyra felt odd having a conversation about a fictional person, and vowed to set things right as soon as she could. Now wasn't really the time to blow their cover. "So that's why you were there, hey?" she said, trying to keep her voice light. "Doing your research?"

"No," he said firmly, eyes locked on hers. "That wasn't why I was there. At least…it wasn't the main reason." She was sure he could hear her swallow. "Listen, there's a story I need to tell you. Maybe at some point tonight, if you get a break or something, maybe we can talk?"

Lyra nodded. "I'd like that a lot."

They held eyes for a long moment, and something in the energy between them changed. The way he was looking at her…it made her want to reach right over and kiss him. She knew her face was on fire, but it didn't matter. He was just as flushed.

"Alex!" A voice pierced the room and Lyra's heart hit the floor as the woman from the restaurant, the beautiful one in the picture she'd studied so often, flung herself at Alex. He grinned, caught her and spun her in a circle. She was wearing a beautiful blood-coloured dress with a plunging neckline and her long dark hair was swept over one shoulder. She was absolutely stunning, even more so up close, and Lyra's heart sank as she realised the woman's dress matched Alex's pocket-square.

Had she imagined what happened just a second ago? Confused and hurt, she turned away from them and walked towards Mick, who was struggling with some cabling.

"Lyra," Alex called, holding his arm around Restaurant Woman's waist. "This is-"

"Sorry, I'm really busy here." Embarrassed at what she

had let myself imagine she cut him off, throwing the merest of glances in their direction.

There was a puzzled silence, then Lyra heard the woman gently say, "Let's leave her. We can try later."

Mick watched Lyra carefully for a moment. "What was that all about?" he asked in a low voice.

She shook her head. Tears were threatening and she didn't trust herself to speak. Tonight, she firmly decided, was purely and simply about wooing the audience with her music. And keeping an eye out for any danger for Mick.

The wedding ceremony was beautiful, short and moving. Even Mick wiped his eye as Lyra had sung the bride towards the groom, who was anxiously waiting under the flower garland, with an abridged version of *Nothing Compares 2U.*

The best man had performed his ring-bearing duties with admirable solemnity and a quivering chin. Lyra was glad she wasn't the only emotional one at this wedding. She'd sneaked the smallest of glimpses at Alex and found him looking at her, his eyes full. He'd given her a sheepish look and sniffed, as the beautiful woman leaned into him. Lyra quickly looked elsewhere, annoyed at herself for having seen them.

Somewhere between second course and dessert, when wine and conversation were flowing around the tables and Lyra and Mick were playing what was more or less background music, Lyra took a good look around at the wedding guests. She hadn't been keen to lift her eyes much - afraid they would catch sight of Alex and the beautiful woman again.

Right in the back, furthest from the stage, there was a table of army men and women. Lyra had seen a few of them arriving, all in very high spirits and in uniform. Lyra watched their table for a while. They seemed like a tight group of old friends who were definitely enjoying the evening. There was one guest with his back to her, who didn't turn at all. Not even slightly to the side, so she could catch the merest glimpse of his profile. Lyra felt a sense of foreboding. She knew that head. Where did she know that head from? The question absorbed her so much she almost missed a cue from Mick. She shook her head and snapped back to reality, softly singing one of the cheesy love songs the couple had requested for the dinner set. Shortly after, Lyra and Mick took a short break and Lyra was coming back from the bathroom with her eyes on the floor when she ran smack into one of the men from the army table.

"Oh, God. Sorry!" she said, and looked up...at a horror-stricken Rick. Lyra instantly realised why the back of the head had looked so familiar. *"What?"*

For a second Rick was unable to answer. Then finally he pulled himself together. "I can explain," he said, sounding desperate.

Lyra narrowed her eyes. "That's good, because I'm going to need one *hell* of an explanation! Amy thinks you work in construction, why have you been lying to her? And don't tell me you're so important that it had to be kept secret."

He shook his head and squeezed his eyes shut. Glancing around, he took Lyra by the arm and led her to a small ante-chamber where the gift table was set up.

"Well?" she said, hands on hips as she faced him.

"I didn't mean for this to happen." He sounded pitiful. "I fell in love with her that very first night. I knew she was special before I even spoke a word to her."

"She *is*," Lyra snapped. "Special enough not to be lied to!"

"I thought...I didn't think..." He took a breath. "That she'd be interested in someone in the army." He looked so miserable that some of Lyra's anger fizzled. He obviously hadn't done this to hurt Amy - wasn't here sneaking around with another woman and a second identity and children. As far as she could tell.

"Why not?" Lyra asked, slightly more gently.

He looked pained. "She basically said so on our very first night, when we saw someone in uniform. It can be hard for partners. We never know if we'll need to move around. I knew she had the kind of career that wouldn't really work with that."

Lyra nodded. "It's definitely a choice your partners need to make. But, Rick, that's the point. It's *their* choice."

He nodded. "Me being in the army...it's been the cause of a few breakups. I knew I couldn't get away with it forever, but it was just so *good* being with her that I somehow let the time slip away." Lyra's heart ached for him. "Then it was too late and I didn't know how to raise it." He looked mournfully at her. "She'll never forgive me when I tell her."

"So you are going to tell her," Lyra said, more stating a fact than asking a question.

He nodded. "I know I messed up. But please do me the favour of letting me tell her myself. I promise I'll do it as soon as I see her again."

They were silent for a moment.

"I can totally see how it happened," Lyra said gently. "I hope she forgives you."

"Do you think there's any chance at all?"

Lyra bit her lip, not wanting to give him false hope. "I know she's in love with you."

His shoulders slumped. She couldn't help herself; she gave him a quick hug and then left the room. She needed to get back to Mick, who was probably either worried she'd fallen down the toilet, or, more likely, had fallen down one himself.

CHAPTER TWENTY-FIVE

I t was dark by the time their set was finished and the dance floor had been handed over to someone's iPad. Roberta briskly ushered them into the same antechamber Lyra had been in earlier, so they could eat their dinner. A small table had been set up and the gifts had been cleared away.

As they sat down and were served a glass of wine each, Lyra saw Alex enter the room shyly, the beautiful woman glued to his side. Her face instantly turned to thunder and she pretended not to see them. She'd managed to block all of that out and yet here he was, bringing the woman in to flaunt in front of her again. She was determined to be made of ice. Whatever Alex was playing at, if he wanted a reaction from her, he wasn't going to get one.

Mick watched them approach, took one look at Lyra's face and stood up to leave.

"Sit," she hissed at him and he dropped obediently back into his seat.

"Lyra?" Alex said tentatively. She pretended to be surprised.

"Oh, hi." She barely glanced in their direction.

"There's someone I'd really like you to meet."

"Hmm?" She sipped her wine. Alex positioned himself in front of her face, his arm still firmly around the woman's waist. She looked anxious.

"This is my cousin, Jenny." He cleared his throat. "She's the real owner of Meat is Murder. And she'll start working there again from Monday."

Instantly, Lyra felt relief and embarrassment flood her body. It took a full moment for his words to sink in and for her to react. She looked helplessly at Mick, who tried to hide an I-told-you-so smile behind his wine glass.

Slowly, Lyra put down her glass and stood up, extending a hand.

"It's really nice to meet you, Jenny."

Jenny grinned and threw her arms around Lyra in an energetic hug that almost toppled her backwards. "I'm glad to finally meet the woman who's been giving Alex such a run for his money!"

"Well, to be fair, I think it's been the other way around," Lyra said, regaining her footing. "What with that lamb and everything."

Jenny turned to Alex. "Lamb?"

"It's a long story." He shook his head at Lyra in a silent plea for her to drop the topic.

At that moment, an older woman entered the room. She had grey-blonde, perfectly-styled hair and was wearing a beautiful navy dress. Her eyes were drawn to Mick, although she spoke to Jenny.

"I've been looking everywhere for you, sweetie."

"Sorry, Mum. What's up?"

"I need your help getting Uncle Derek away from Aunt Merry."

Jenny groaned and looked at the three of them apologetically. Mick's eyes were riveted to the lady, so Lyra did some hasty introductions. "Does everyone recognise Mick? The better half of the band? Everyone, Mick. Mick, this is Alex, Jenny and... I'm sorry, I didn't catch your name."

"Kathryn," she said, bypassing Lyra to stretch her hand out to Mick. He stood and kissed it gallantly.

"It's wonderful to meet you, Kathryn," he said, as their eyes locked.

There was an awkward silence in the room as Lyra, Alex and Jenny exchanged amused glances. Then Jenny pulled lightly on her mother's other hand. "Let's go avert this crisis, shall we?"

Once they had left, Alex turned to Mick. "Do you mind if I borrow her for a moment? Won't be long."

"Take her as long as you like. Can finally read my paper in peace that way," he said, pulling the broadsheet out.

"Where were you keeping that?" Lyra asked. He wiggled his eyebrows like it was a magic trick and, laughing, they left him.

The sand was cool beneath their bare feet as they walked away from the surf house and towards the dunes. Lyra pulled her shawl around her shoulders, admiring the full moon's glittering path across the black water. The waves broke rhythmically along the shore, and the air was misty with salt.

Lyra had often wished she lived on the west coast, just to watch the sunset over the sea, but right now she decided moon-rise was just as beautiful.

"I wouldn't call it lying," Alex said, walking so closely beside her that their arms brushed. "More like...omission."

Lyra let out a short laugh. "That the truck doesn't belong

to you and never did and you're a carnivore and the woman from the restaurant is your cousin and the real owner?" She shoved him playfully and he held his hands up in surrender, grinning. "Yeah, I guess that's an omission."

They walked in silence for a moment. "I'm really sorry."

Lyra looked up at him and his smile sent her heart haywire. "I know I flipped out a little at the beginning, but Silas and I had been through a really horrible turf war in the city. And it seemed like we were about to go through that again."

He stopped suddenly and turned to her. "I honestly didn't mean to frighten you. If I'd known what you'd been through…" He shook his head. "I feel like an idiot now."

"What were you doing with that insane sandwich board though?"

"Oh, God," he groaned, palming his forehead. "One of Jenny's suppliers sent that to her. I found it in the truck and I don't even really know what I was thinking, putting it out. It was dumb, but I wasn't really thinking too straight. I'm sorry about that, too."

Lyra grinned. "This is becoming a pretty repetitive conversation."

He laughed. "Yeah. The thing is…I was just supposed to take over the truck until Jenny recovered from a really severe lung infection. I was going through the stuff with Alison and it seemed like it might be a good way to get my mind off things. Jenny had also finally got her permits for the spot next to you at Lilac Bay, and she didn't want to jeopardise that by not turning up. She asked me not to tell people the truck wasn't mine. The licence is only under her name and I didn't have the proper training at the beginning." He stopped and held up his palm. "I do now though, before you call the authorities."

Lyra laughed. They were quite far from the surf house now. Occasionally, a laugh or a snatch of conversation floated to them across the sand. Otherwise, they were completely alone. "Just supposed to stay until she got better, huh?" Lyra said. "What happened?"

They stopped and he looked her in the eye. Her breath quickened and her heart rate picked up. "A toddler almost fell into the harbour and a beautiful girl rushed out to save her. And once I'd met her, I really wasn't in a hurry to leave. Even if I did think she was taken." He looked down at the sand, tracing a line in it with his big toe.

Lyra took several breaths to steady herself as a huge wave of emotion rolled over her. She wanted to be sure she understood what he was saying. "Alex, you told me you aren't in a place to start anything-" she began and he looked up.

"I wanted to make sure I wasn't rushing into anything and I needed to process what happened. The truth is that Alison and I were a bad match, we always were. We tried to stay together because at some point it was just easier. But when she cheated with that Miles guy from the bar-"

The rest of his words faded as Lyra's blood rang in her ears. She felt a wave of nausea sweep over her. *Miles.* Alison had cheated on Alex with *Miles.* It had to be the same Miles, surely. The thoughts came fast. Should she say something now? What if that made Alex change his mind about her? It had taken them so long to get to this point. And nothing had really happened with Miles. Nothing serious, anyway. Still, she should say something…she just couldn't find the words.

Alex was looking at her. "Did you hear what I said?" he asked gently. "You look like you're in another world."

"Sorry," she said quickly. Without thinking, she laid a hand on his arm and he looked down at it. "What did you say?"

He drew a deep breath. "I said I realise now that I'm fully over what happened with Alison. I'm ready to start something new…"

He was watching her intently, his gaze smouldering. Lyra's stomach fluttered and all she wanted was to pull him to her and feel his lips on hers. But not like this. Not when she was so off-kilter. She didn't want to be distracted for their first kiss.

She took a deep breath and looked up at him. "Now I need a moment," she said, her voice quivering. "Can we keep walking for a bit?"

"Yes, of course," he said, with slightly forced brightness. They walked in silence for a moment, directionless among the dunes. "Your parents must be so proud of you and Silas," Alex said suddenly, changing the subject. "Running your own business and everything."

Lyra snorted and he looked quizzically at her. "We haven't seen or spoken to our father for more years than I can count."

His face fell. "Do you want to talk about it?" he asked gently.

Lyra shrugged. "Our mother died of cancer when we were both small, actually the anniversary is in a couple of weeks. My dad was an alcoholic who got remarried to someone who…hated us. And she was very religious." Lyra turned to look at him and he was watching her intently. She felt unhurried. She felt like what she said was important. She realised this was everything Mick had told her to look out for that day in his garage when he'd given her relationship advice. She felt completely like herself.

"Then he turned religious too," Lyra continued. "They kicked Silas out of the house when he told them he was gay." She laughed tonelessly. "Threw all his stuff on the lawn like it was garbage, changed the locks and left an envelope on the doorstep addressed to me. The new key was inside."

"Whoa," Alex said softly and Lyra nodded sadly.

"Of course I shoved the envelope into the letterbox and I followed Silas. We just walked away, started again with nothing but a few things we took from the pile. That was the last we saw of them. The last we wanted to see of them."

Alex took a moment to process this news, then shook his head angrily. "I will never understand parents disowning their children for being themselves."

"I don't get it either."

"I'll bet your mother is crazy proud of you, wherever she is."

Unexpectedly, a sob escaped her. Her mother had been on her mind so much lately. It was nice to hear those words, because it was true. But they had no one to tell them that. Their mother had always been proud of them and, just as Alex had said, wherever she was, she was proud of them now. Unable to stop the tears, Lyra gave into them. She sat down hard in the sand and hugged her legs into her chest.

Alex sat close beside her and tentatively slipped an arm around her shoulder. He gave her the pocket square from his suit and she dabbed at her eyes and nose. She leaned into him and they stayed that way for a long time, long after her tears had stopped.

Once she was sure she was steady enough to speak, Lyra blew her nose one final time and stood up, dusting the sand off. "Thank you. You must be desperate to get back to the wedding."

He stood up beside her and gently slipped a finger under her chin when she couldn't bring herself to look up. "Lyra, no I'm not. I could sit here forever with you…"

He brushed the remains of her tears from her cheeks, hesitating as though he wasn't sure it was the right time to make a move. She tilted her head towards him, closing her eyes.

"Lyra! Alex!" The voice cut down the beach and shattered the moment. They both turned to see Jenny racing towards them, her red dress flying out behind her. They shared a panicked look and then wordlessly broke into a run to try and meet her halfway. It must surely have to do with Mick. But what could possibly have gone wrong? Lyra had left him sitting in a carpeted dining room!

When they reached her, Jenny was breathless. She doubled over as she tried to catch her breath.

"Mick?" Lyra asked.

She nodded. "Allergic reaction. Ambulance just left."

"To what?"

Jenny shrugged. "Shellfish? Something."

"Why did he eat if he was allergic?" Lyra asked, knowing Jenny couldn't possibly answer that.

"My mum's gone with him in the ambulance."

"Which hospital are they going to?" Lyra asked, breaking into a run to get back to the surf house. They were too far from home for him to go to his local hospital, so at least Lyra wouldn't risk running into Alison. She wasn't sure she could have handled that right now. Alex ran beside her.

"I wish I hadn't been drinking," Alex said ruefully. "I'd drive you."

"I asked the bus driver," Jenny panted, trying to keep up. "He'll take you to the hospital."

"I'm coming," Alex said.

"You can't leave a family wedding," Lyra argued. They reached the surf house and struggled up the steps. "Especially since the keyboard player made such a dramatic exit."

"They took him out the back door," Jenny said. "No one wanted the bride to worry. People are pretty drunk so I don't think they noticed."

"Oh, thank God," Lyra said, relieved. Maybe they could salvage something of this after all. She had no idea how they'd pack up our equipment and get it back.

As if reading her mind, Alex said, "I'll help you get your stuff, whatever you need, let's just get going."

CHAPTER TWENTY-SIX

"I feel like I've spent half my life in hospital waiting rooms," Lyra said as Alex handed her a third paper cup of questionable coffee. She was being eyed by a worn-out looking man sitting opposite them in the waiting room. He was grinding his teeth, fiddling with his keys, using jerky movements and radiating a strange, restless aggression.

"Mick's a pretty lucky guy," Alex said, eyeing the man opposite them and scooting almost imperceptibly closer to Lyra. Her heart swelled at the subconscious display of protection.

"Silas thinks he's unlucky."

Alex shrugged, "He's survived it all. That seems pretty lucky to me."

"That's what I think."

They sat in comfortable silence for a moment, then Lyra felt his hand touch hers, brushing against it gently. They slowly wound their pinky fingers around each other. A moment later, both still facing straight ahead, they laced all their fingers and sat holding hands. Lyra's heart was racing and a slow smile was spreading over her face. She was too overwhelmed to make eye contact with Alex and wondered whether he was smiling too. Her question was answered seconds later.

"What are youse two grinning like idiots about?" the man opposite them said, getting up and stalking to a different section of the waiting area. They exploded into laughter and at that moment, a young woman wearing scrubs and crocs came out and looked hesitantly into the waiting room, reading from a clipboard.

"Lee...Leerah Beck? Is there a Leerah Beck here?" she asked timidly.

Lyra stood up, reluctantly dropping Alex's hand.

"Wait." He grabbed it back. "I need your number."

Lyra was about to repeat it by rote when she froze, remembering it was Margot's number too. A number he'd called. A number he would have saved in his phone. There wasn't time to explain, not right before she had to leave him. She hesitated for so long that the smile began to fade from his face. He gently let go of her hand.

"Stop," she said, trying to think fast. She blurted out Silas's number in a moment of panic.

"Is there a Leerah Beck here, please?" the young woman repeated more loudly.

"Yes!" Lyra said, holding up her arm. "It's *Lye-rah*, but yes, I'm here." She turned back to Alex. "Four three eight eight," she repeated as he typed quickly into his phone.

"I can wait for you here," he said. "I don't mind."

She shook her head. "I'm going to stay with Mick for a while and Silas will pick me up. Besides, you should get back to the wedding."

He nodded and Lyra followed the nurse out of the waiting room. Just before rounding the corner, she turned back to look at Alex. They grinned at each other and her heart hammered. She would need to explain to Silas as soon as possible and just hope that in the meantime the man she liked didn't end up in a sexting exchange with her brother.

CHAPTER TWENTY-SEVEN

Lyra was a swirl of emotions when she woke up on Sunday after the wedding. She was relieved Mick was going to be fine, but explaining the phone situation to Silas in the car ride home had been mortifying. Whenever she thought about Alex and their almost-kiss, her stomach did flip flops. She couldn't wait to see him again at Lilac Bay the next day, although it was going to be strange with Jenny there as well. If she could text him, she would ask how much longer he was going to be there for, but Silas was being odd about her using his phone and she didn't want to push her luck.

Overwhelmingly, Lyra was worried about Amy. She picked up her phone a thousand times during the day to call Amy and talk, but each time she stopped, remembering the look on Rick's face. Lyra didn't want to interfere in their relationship and maybe, by some miracle, Rick could find a way to tell Amy the truth in a way that didn't break them up. But Lyra knew in her heart there was no chance of it and was on tenterhooks waiting for Amy's call.

On Monday morning, on their way to open The Pie-ganic, Silas held out a text message to Lyra. It was a short one from Alex letting her know he wouldn't be at Lilac Bay that day as he had to help his mother with some errands. Lyra nodded and sighed, taking Silas' cell and typing a quick message back. She wished she hadn't got herself into this stupid mess with the phones. She had been planning to tell Alex about the silly situation face-to-face that day. It would need to wait, again. Margot had been a bad idea from the beginning, although Lyra had to admit she'd given a big boost to the number of enquiries and bookings she and Mick got.

Jenny arrived at Lilac Bay to open Meat is Murder at around the same time as them and Lyra hugged her, doing a quick round of introductions with Silas.

The day dragged for Lyra. Early in the afternoon, Amy sent a text to her and Marley asking them to come to her place that night, saying she was in desperate need of them. Lyra knew then that Rick had told her and that Amy hadn't forgiven him. It was over between them. Her heart ached. For her friend, and also for Rick. Lyra of all people knew how easily a little white lie could snowball. Maybe there was a chance she could convince Amy that evening.

As soon as they shuttered the truck, Lyra walked to the little flower store near the ferry terminal and bought a huge bunch of flowers. She met Marley outside Amy's place. Marley was lugging a shopping bag filled with enough chocolate to choke a horse.

Amy hugged them wordlessly at the door, dark circles beneath her eyes. Her face was pale and makeup free. They'd never seen her like this and shared a look of concern. Amy was in her pyjamas - which of course were silk - and over which she wore a stylish leopard-print dressing gown paired with white lambskin slippers. But her spark was gone and it was unmistakable and heart-breaking.

Amy fixed the three of them cocktails, Lyra and Marley holding stilted conversation while she did so. Then they stood around as Amy twirled her metal straw in the copper mug, not saying a word.

Amy's rotary phone rang and she walked straight to the wall and yanked it out by the plug, returning to stir her barely-touched cocktail in silence.

Marley cleared her throat. "Ames...What can we do?"

Amy lifted her eyes sadly to them. "Let me wallow," she said softly.

Lyra heaved a sigh. She was hurting for Amy, knowing how hard her friend had fallen for Rick. And she was hurting for Rick, too. She cleared her throat, and the look on her face must have tipped Marley off as to what she was about to say. Marley sensed no good could come of it, widening her eyes at Lyra and shaking her head slightly. Lyra ploughed ahead, regardless. "Amy, he only did it because he wanted you to get to know him without any bias."

Amy's head snapped up. "So, by lying to me," she said, so aggressively that Lyra winced and Marley looked away. "By creating an entire fake identity and completely misrepresenting everything he is and everything he stands for. Knowing full well how I would feel about his career, he continued to dupe me."

"Dupe is a strong-"

"That's what it was!" Amy said hotly. "Lyra, are you seriously trying to defend him?"

Lyra was silent for a moment, biting her lip. "It's just that someone could say the same thing to me about Margot. And she was your idea, with the very best of intent-"

Amy slammed her mug on the counter. "Who's side are you on?" she demanded, her eyes hot. Lyra looked down at her cocktail, wishing for a second she could disappear into its depths.

"Sorry," she mumbled. "Just wanted to give you a different perspective."

"There isn't one," Amy said, softening slightly.

An awkward silence fell.

"How is Mick?" Marley asked.

"I get déjà vu whenever I hear that question." Amy rolled her eyes.

"Don't we all." Lyra tried to force a smile. "He's good. Turns out he has an allergy to shellfish that he never knew about. He's never eaten it before because he didn't like the look of it."

"Why did he start that night?" Marley asked.

"He fancied Alex's aunt Kathryn and she was sitting by him. He didn't want to seem fussy, he thought it would be unmanly."

"So instead his whole head swelled up, he turned purple and had to be taken away in an ambulance?" Amy asked. "Very manly."

"Seems to have worked though," Lyra said. "Kathryn was the one who drove him home after his discharge."

"Well, it's one way to meet a partner I guess!" Amy said.

"Alex took me to the hospital." As soon as the words were out of her mouth, Lyra regretted it. This wasn't the time to be rubbing budding romances in Amy's face.

"What's going on with you two?" Marley asked. Amy looked away.

"Nothing yet." Lyra's face reddened.

Amy heaved a sigh, and Lyra felt useless in the face of Amy's heartbreak. She had no idea how to make her feel better. Especially since she truly believed Rick deserved a second chance. But then, what was the point if Amy didn't want a partner in the army? It was just heart-breaking that two people who obviously loved each other should be kept apart.

Lyra and Marley watched Amy, who slowly stirred her drink.

"Shall we maybe put on some music and dance?" Marley suggested.

"I'm not in the mood," Amy said, without looking up.

"Oh. Well, too bad because I am." Marley got off her stool, rooted around in the record collection and laid Dolly Parton's *Here You Come Again* on the player. Then she began to dance, extremely awkwardly.

She was wearing what could only be described as a muumuu, overlaid with a bright orange cardigan and teamed with a giant set of plush rabbit-head slippers. She'd had them in her bag specially to wear at Amy's. She looked completely and utterly ridiculous and Lyra had never loved her more.

Amy watched her in stony-faced silence for a moment. Then she looked at Lyra with the hint of a smile in her eyes.

A small part of Lyra was jealous that Marley had been the one to find a temporary solution to Amy's sadness, but she got up off her stool and began to dance alongside Marley, making her moves even clunkier and more awkward. They descended into a kind of bad-taste dance-off,and before long the corners of Amy's mouth were twitching. She didn't join in dancing, but Lyra felt like they were getting somewhere.

"You guys are nuts," Amy said after a while, shaking her head and finally letting herself laugh.

When Lyra's alarm went off in the morning, her mouth was dusty and she had a pounding headache. She groaned, throwing her arm up to shelter her eyes from the overhead light in her room, which she'd left on.

She had no idea what time she'd come home, only that Silas had eventually had to get up and open the front door for her after she struggled for so long to get the key in the lock.

When she could finally sit up without feeling nauseous, she drank down the glass of water on her nightstand and looked around the room. Her clothes were strewn everywhere and her handbag was maddeningly just out of reach. She was in need of an aspirin and she knew she had a blister pack in the front pocket.

"Silas," she called weakly. There was no response.

She groaned and dragged herself out of bed, snatching up the handbag. She quickly laid back down to fight off a fresh wave of nausea. With her eyes closed, she shoved a hand into her bag and rooted around for the tablets. She caught hold of a sheet of paper, and pulled it out. A scrawled note read: *Lyra Muck, gog house band 14 sweet, bleg. 11 wed, 19th. BOTH.*

"What the…?" She studied it for a long while, turning it this way and that, but had absolutely no memory of having written it. Surely, she wouldn't have referred to herself in third person? Amy had the handwriting of a classically-trained calligraphist from heaven, so there was only one person who could have written this note.

Lyra dialled her number and Marley answered on the sixth ring.

"Shhhhh," she croaked into the phone. "I feel like my head's made of glass. Please whisper."

"Oh, that's fine with me," Lyra replied softly.

"You should be used to this. I basically never drink so this has hit me…hard."

"Yeah. I'm not doing too well either, I'm going to admit. I don't know how I'm going to work today. Listen," she said, lying flat on her back with the phone wedged between shoulder and ear as she held the note up. "Did you write a note last night? Did you answer a call on my phone?"

Marley drew some long, shaky breaths. "Sorry," she said

finally, "I thought I was going to be sick. Uh, I think so? Maybe…wait a second. I think I pretended to be Margot."

"What?" Lyra screeched, and recoiled from the noise as Marley groaned. "Oh my God, I'm so sorry."

"I'm never drinking again for the rest of my life. I don't even care if there's a gun to my head."

"Why would someone hold a gun to…never mind." Lyra closed her eyes. "You pretended to be Margot? Did you do the accent?"

There was a long pause. "She was Irish, right?"

Lyra groaned. "No, she's from England."

"Are you sure?"

"Yeah. Well…so they might think she's a bit eccentric. Unless they've never spoken to her before." Lyra broke off to heave herself onto her elbow and take another sip of water, before flopping back down. "The problem is I can't understand much of your writing."

"Yeah. It's bad. My teacher used to call it chicken scratch at school."

"That was a generous teacher." They both laughed and then sighed with pain.

"It does come in handy with the doctor though. I can read her writing at times when I don't even think the FBI could."

"So, I get that it says Lyra and Mick…then it appears to say *gog house band*. Does that ring a bell?"

"Do the words gog house band in a sentence ring a bell?" Marley asked. "No. No they do not."

"Oh, Marley, I have no idea what you wrote. Do you remember anything about it?"

She paused. "I do remember that it was exciting and that it seemed like really good news."

"Okay, well that's…nothing we can work with."

"Yeah. Listen, why don't you take a picture of it and text it to me."

"There's no name or number on it though."

"Oh."

"Did you take a name or number?"

Marley paused. "Could Gog House Band be a person's name?"

"I very seriously doubt that," Lyra said, chuckling. "Okay, I need to go and die now, so I'll send you the picture. I hope you can tell me what it means."

Lyra snapped a pic of the note, texting it to Marley along with multiple question marks.

She heard the front door open. "Si?"

"It's me." She heard rustling and he appeared in her doorway.

"My head hurts," she groaned.

"You sound like you've been smoking since you were a toddler." He chuckled.

Lyra gave him her most self-pitying look and he threw a paper bag at her. It landed heavily near her torso.

"What's in that?"

"A bacon and egg roll. You're welcome. And here's a latte macchiato." He laid a coffee cup on her nightstand.

"I could actually kiss you if it wasn't illegal. You're the best brother in the world."

"I'm going to go in. You just come when you can."

"Thanks."

"Oh, and I have another surprise for you."

"Please don't make me guess," she whispered.

"Your boyfriend has been texting you." He held his phone up with a grin. She squinted and he brought it closer. On the screen were a few messages from Alex. "And he's *interested.*"

CHAPTER TWENTY-EIGHT

Lyra finally dragged herself out of bed an hour later, taking a quick shower and gulping as much water as she could. On her way into Lilac Bay, she opened her maps app, looking for all the Sweet Streets in the surrounding area, checking them one by one to see what was at number 14.

The nearest was a butcher, which would have made sense if it was about the food truck but made none if it was about her singing. The second seemed to be a residential address and the third was a church. Scrolling to the fourth in the list, Lyra felt a shiver run down her spine.

14 Sweet Street, *Bligh*, was home to a record label. Teller's Music. Was it possible they had a meeting there? Lyra texted Marley to see whether that sounded familiar.

Maybe? she replied and Lyra tried to contain her excitement. The next day was the 19th but Lyra wasn't sure whether the month was right. Whoever had called last night had done so from a private number, so she couldn't double check without ringing Teller's Music and potentially making a fool of herself and appearing unprofessional. She decided to tell Mick, take some time off from The Pie-ganic and both turn up to the address at 11. Worst case scenario, the record company would have no idea why she and Mick were there.

Alex and Jenny were in Meat is Murder when she arrived. She exchanged shy smiles with Alex and a quick wave with Jenny, then headed straight to The Pie-ganic to help Silas with the long line.

Between customers, Lyra commandeered Silas's phone, exchanging a long stream of texts with Alex. Little observations about people walking along Lilac Bay, about the screams from the amusement park, or when they thought they saw Reg and Lucinda walking past. It was driving Silas mad and he pocketed his phone.

"Oh, I just thought of something I need to tell him," Lyra said. "Can I just have it one more time?"

"No." Silas shook his head. "He's so close you could throw a pie at him. Just go over there and explain what's going on. It's ridiculous, you're being a child."

"But there's no way to explain without me sounding like an idiot," Lyra said, hating the whine in her voice.

"You heard what you just said, right?"

"Come on, Si, *one* more-"

"No! The jig is up." He pocketed it firmly and busied himself tidying the condiments.

She crossed her arms and leaned huffily against the counter. "I saw the message from Ernie."

Silas's cheeks grew heated, but he refused to give her a reaction. "Can you be legally emancipated from a sibling?" he asked, deadpan. Then his mouth quirked and they burst out laughing. "Just go talk to Alex, will you? You're being pathetic and you're annoying me. Aren't you supposed to be a modern woman? March over there and ask him out."

"A *modern woman*? What is this, the twenties?"

Silas shrugged but their exchange reminded Lyra how

bad she felt for Amy. She and Rick were so in love, now they couldn't be together. She was doing the exact same thing to herself.

Before she could think better of it, she slipped off her apron and wandered over to Alex's truck. Jenny was inside and Alex was standing outside, talking to Jogging Lady. She was apparently on a break, leaning casually up against the truck with her arms folded. She laughed at something Alex said and Lyra's resolve withered. She spun on her heel. Alex spotted her and excused himself from Jogging Lady.

"Lyra, wait!" he said, walking over to her and smiling. Her heart skipped a beat. How had she ever looked at this man without her stomach doing flip flops?

"You didn't reply to my last text," he said in a low voice, once he was near her. She breathed in the scent of him. "We only have a week left of being in the same beautiful surroundings together." He gestured around at the bay.

"Uh, my phone smashed."Looking into his grey eyes, she simply couldn't bring herself to tell him the ridiculous truth.

"Ah, that's too bad!" He scuffed the toe of his sneaker on the ground and was about to stick his hands in his pockets when he stopped himself.

Now or never, Lyra said to herself. She took a deep breath, and in that exact same moment, he spoke. "Want to go on a date?" she asked, as he said, "I've been meaning to ask-

"Sorry, what did you say?" he asked, leaning in.

Her heart was hammering so loudly she was sure he could hear it.

"No, what were you going to say?"

He grinned. "I wasn't saying anything. Did you mention a date? Lyra, did you ask me on a date?"

She squeezed her eyes closed, then raised her chin to look him square in the eye. He was grinning cheekily at her.

"Forget it!" She swatted him and pretended to walk away. He took two quick steps after her and wrapped his arms around her. She froze as he tilted his head to hers, so close she could feel the heat of his skin.

"I thought you'd never ask," he whispered in her ear and her breath came ragged. "And I was about to ask you the same thing."

It was all Lyra could do not to kiss him right there on the promenade - with Jogging Lady and Silas pretending not to gawk.

"I've been planning a date in my head for a while. I'll pick you up at your place at six thirty. I already got your address off Silas this morning."

Lyra turned to look at her brother, who waved joyfully. She would kill him later. Maybe after finally getting him to realise he liked Ernie.

"Well," Lyra said, turning back to Alex and looking deep into his eyes. "I guess you can't text me if you change your mind."

He smiled and pulled her close to whisper into her ear. "Oh, I won't change my mind. I've been waiting for this for far too long."

Lyra suddenly felt very warm despite the coolness of the day.

❖

Silas agreed to let Lyra head home early so she could squeeze in a recovery nap before Alex picked her up. As she stood in front of the bathroom mirror getting ready, she heard Silas come home. She was a bundle of nerves and had tried on at least six outfits. Not having any idea what they'd be doing, she'd chosen a fool-proof jeans and jumper combo, with a thick, peach-coloured jacket rolled up in her bag in case it got really cold.

"Where are you guys going?" Silas asked, appearing behind her.

"I know nothing except that he told me to dress warm."

Silas nodded. "I bet he's taking you to mini golf."

She laughed. "No!"

"Mushroom picking, then. Or to an all-you-can-eat buffet."

"Are these actual dates you've been on?" Silas smiled, but didn't answer.

Lyra slicked on some lipstick, then immediately wiped it off. In the best case scenario it would be smeared across two faces. The thought made her smile. Silas watched her from behind, both their faces reflected in the glass.

"Are you okay with this, Si?" She turned to him. "I know you were interested in him for a moment."

Silas laughed. "I just liked looking at him. And I'm sorry to tell you, that's not going to change." Lyra grinned. "Are you going to tell him about Margot tonight?"

"Is Ernie coming over?" she countered and watched his face closely. For an instant, it lit up. Then the mask of nonchalance reappeared. He shrugged casually.

"I told him I was home tonight. If he wants to swing by, he can. No biggie."

"Why can't you admit that you like him?"

"Because I don't." He held her gaze and as it struck her again how beautiful he was, a thought occurred to her.

"You don't think he's good-looking enough for you?"

Silas actually blushed. "Honestly, do you think I'm that shallow?"

A slow grin spread over her face. "Yes!" she said finally. "I do. And I know the kind of guys you usually date. Adonises with less brains than a wheel of cheese. Oh, Silas. You're denying yourself a relationship with an awesome guy just because you think you're hotter than him!"

Silas finally shrugged. "I'm not saying that's the case, but so what if it was? You don't know he's awesome, you've only spoken to him a couple of times. I'm still making my mind up about him and attraction is a huge part of life, sorry to tell you. Besides, how long did it take you to realise you were into Alex?"

"That's different!"

"How so?"

"I'm running late so I can't get into it," she said, laughing. Silas hmphed at her and went to leave. He turned back.

"You're an absolute pain in the bum but you look really pretty. I hope you have a great night tonight."

She crossed the bathroom before he could escape and hugged him tightly. "Thank you. I hope you do too."

On her way out, she kissed her fingers and pressed them to her mother's picture. This was the kind of moment Lyra wished desperately to share with her, the kind of moment she could imagine her mother getting Very Excited about. Just like Lyra was.

CHAPTER TWENTY-NINE

"**Y**ou know, you're totally squashing my fake lashes," Lyra said as Alex drove them to the undisclosed location. Despite the blindfold he'd asked her to wear for the last five minutes of the trip, she was relaxed. The evening was milder than the forecast had predicted, and they even had one of the windows down to let in some of the fresh evening air.

"Really?" Alex asked, sounding concerned.

"No! I tried those once and glued my eyes together. Silas didn't stop laughing for a week. I only use mascara now. But are we there yet?"

"I told you to take a bathroom break before we left!" he joked. "But yes, we're just about there."

"Can I hear an aeroplane?"

"Maaaybe." There was a note of humour in his voice.

"Are you smuggling me out of the country? Is that the surprise?" He laughed but didn't say anything else. "You should know, I didn't pack my passport," she added as the car came to a halt. He pulled up the handbrake and cut the engine.

"You won't need it." Alex was unexpectedly close to her ear and the closeness of his voice made her shiver. He opened his door, got out and ran to her side to help her out, insisting the blindfold remain.

"Are you curious?" he asked.

"Not at all," she lied as she gingerly swung her legs out of the car. They didn't walk far, Lyra taking tiny, deer-like steps as he gently held her arm. She thought it was highly unlikely that he was about to throw her off a cliff, but she wasn't at her most rational when blindfolded.

"What's your best guess?"

She wracked her brain. All that came up were places she'd previously been on dates. Movie theatres, restaurants and once, notably... "It's not a funeral, is it?" she joked.

"Okay, so *that's* a story I need to hear. But no, not even close."

He whisked off the blindfold and Lyra blinked as her eyes slowly adjusted. Parked in front of them, lit up by fairy lights, was the Meat is Murder truck. Lyra was momentarily thrown, seeing it away from the usual surroundings at Lilac Bay. A grinning Jenny waved to them from inside.

"I realised that in all this time, you'd never actually tasted Jenny's food," Alex said when Lyra turned to him in delighted surprise. "It's really amazing, so you just have to. Wait a sec."

He led her behind the car and opened the boot to reveal everything they'd need for a picnic. A wicker basket, a quilted picnic blanket, two throws to keep them warm, and a good bottle of red wine.

He pointed slightly beyond the food truck. "I thought we could eat the food as a picnic, unless it gets too cold. Over there is as close as you can get to the runway. It's a small private airfield, and I love coming here at night and watching the planes take off and land." He grew almost shy for a moment. "I kind of thought it might be something you'd like too."

"Alex, this is awesome," Lyra said, beaming. She felt lit up from inside. "I absolutely love this idea." He looked relieved. "I just have one concern," she added, and he raised an eyebrow expectantly. "Is Jenny staying with us the whole night?"

He laughed and then shook his head, smiling at her. "It's just you, me, some braised tofu and alfalfa sprouts and about three hundred tonnes of jet fuel."

"It's every girl's dream."

With the raised car boot sheltering them from Jenny's view, it suddenly felt like they were the only two people in the world. Alex was looking down at her, a half-smile playing on his lips, those grey-gold eyes trained on hers. She took a small step towards him, closing the gap between them, never taking her eyes from his.

He gently reached his hand out to touch her face and stroked her cheek. Then he leaned towards her, slipping his hand behind her neck to pull her face close. Lyra's heart was racing as he grazed his lips over hers, slowly and teasingly until she couldn't wait any longer. Lyra grabbed him and kissed him, hard. His lips were soft and it felt like her entire body was full of electricity. Her mind went blank as he wrapped his arms tightly around her and she lost all track of time. They only broke apart, breathless, when Jenny whistled.

"I know what you're doing behind there!" she yelled. Alex's torso had become fiery against Lyra's.

They laughed a little and he leaned his cheek on top of her head in mock embarrassment. How different this whole moment was from the encounter with Miles in the bathroom. Right now, Lyra couldn't believe she'd ever found Miles attractive.

They made their way to the food truck and Jenny greeted them happily.

"It's so good to see you again, Lyra. And you, cuz." She leaned forward and pecked Alex on the cheek. "You're a little late, even later after the show you just put on, and I need to drive this thing to an event. So what'll it be?"

Alex laughed. "Don't pretend we have a choice and that you haven't already prepared something for us!"

Jenny winked at Lyra, then turned to grab their food. She handed them four cartons.

"I made you two different things so you can share. A sweet chilli tofu bowl with seasonal veg and herbs. And pasta shells stuffed with butternut pumpkin and cashew cheese. And for dessert, one lemongrass coconut custard and a peanut butter cookie bar."

"Wow!" Lyra exclaimed, peeking into one of the boxes. "This smells absolutely amazing." She looked back and forth between them. "I can't believe your truck hasn't run us out of business."

Jenny smiled. "There are two reasons. One, my cousin was kind of a jerk when he first arrived."

"I won't argue," Lyra said, elbowing Alex playfully.

"And two, Alex told me the regulars just love you and your brother. They never want to go anywhere else. A lot of them think of you as a kind of extended work family."

Lyra grinned at Alex. "You mean Frank, right?"

He laughed. "Frank is hot competition! But really, it's not just him. You guys create a good atmosphere. People *really* like you. Half of Lilac Bay call you guys 'the hot brother and sister.'"

"Well," Lyra said, unable to wipe a slightly goofy grin off her face. "No one tell Silas that!" They laughed and Lyra looked back up at Jenny. "I can't believe it's taken me this long to try your food, but it looks and smells incredible."

"I look forward to your feedback - one food truckie to another. Now, the two of you scram. I gotta split."

They hugged her goodbye and walked to a little clearing with a great view of the runway.

Alex spread out the picnic blanket and pulled a lantern out of the wicker basket. He struck a match to light it as Lyra settled down and made herself comfortable. He opened the wine bottle and placed two mugs onto the blanket.

"I'm supposed to drink my wine out of this?" she said, in mock outrage. "Where's my cut crystal?"

Alex laughed and laid out cutlery for them, before opening two of the food boxes and sitting down beside her. She scooted into him a little so their bodies were just touching, then took a forkful of the sweet chilli tofu bowl.

"Oh my *God*," she said, through a mouthful of food. Alex smiled.

"She's clever, isn't she?" He forked a pasta shell into his mouth.

"Crazy clever. Wow. This is a beautiful place," Lyra added, looking around. "I never even knew it existed."

They were in a clearing among a small copse of trees that surrounded them almost completely. The clearing gave way to a path that was thickly carved through the trees and headed directly to the runway. They were positioned at the exact spot where the planes lifted from the ground, or touched back down, and their view of the sky was unobstructed above the trees. It felt like another kind of secret garden.

"I love watching the planes take-off and landing and imagining where they're going," he said.

"Well, that one's smuggling drugs in," Lyra said, pointing as a small plane came in to land.

"Probably," he agreed. "It's a Cessna Skyhawk so it's likely also a learner pilot on their first smuggling run. Adrenaline overload."

"You know all the plane types?" Lyra asked, taking a pasta shell. The food really was incredible, Jenny was a genius.

"Would it impress you if I did?" he said, leaning past her to take a bite from the tofu bowl. It was as though his body radiated heat and Lyra's responded when he came near. Like waving a magnet over some iron filings.

"Sure," she shrugged, swallowing hard to try and keep her pulse down.

"Damn. Because that's the only one I remember." He poured a little wine into the mugs and handed her one. "There was a time when I wanted to become a pilot, so I learned all about the types of craft."

She thought of the "Flight Club" email address he'd given Margot. It made sense now. "What stopped you?" she asked, clinking her mug against his. Their eyes held as they both took a sip.

"Colour blindness." He shrugged sadly.

"Oh, I'm so sorry. I can't believe this hasn't come up during all our conversations." She put her mug down, struggling to find the words. "If I felt like I do about singing and I had, I don't know, a frog voice or something, that would have been really, really hard."

He threw his head back and laughed. "A frog voice!"

"It could have happened!" she said, mock defensively. Then she realised something. "I don't actually know what kind of work you do. I know it's not a really interesting question, but I'd like to know."

"It's *very* interesting." He raised his eyebrows. "Have you ever heard of pornography?"

"Shut up!" she laughed, punching him.

He chuckled. "No, I'm an industrial designer. I was working for a homewares company when they downsized.

But...I think I lost my sense of purpose. I really don't know what I want my next step to be. I hope that doesn't make me sound like a flake."

Lyra shook her head. "Not at all. I get it. I think having a sense of purpose is the main thing, right?"

"Yes," he agreed. "Do you get that from your singing?"

Lyra mulled the question, taking a sip of wine. "Yes. When I'm singing, I don't know, it feels..." she struggled for the words. "It feels like the reason I was made."

He put his mug down and turned so that he was facing her. "I liked you the moment I saw you, but when I heard you sing..." he shook his head. "I was done for."

Lyra gulped. "Really?" Her voice came out an octave higher than she intended. She faced him front on.

He nodded firmly. "Yep. I swear to you that once I heard your voice, even if you had looked like Kermit himself, I would have been interested in you. It sort of helped that I also thought you were hot."

She couldn't help but grin at those words. She'd had men tell her things like that in the past of course, but it had rarely felt sincere. This time it did, and it was giving her butterflies...

"But...then I found out you were taken," Alex added.

Lyra shook her head. "Silas only said that because he was jealous. There was never a relationship. It was just a few texts and barely more than that. And it's long over," she added in case there was any doubt.

Alex smiled. "If only I'd known back then."

"But this was better. We got to know each other so much more, without any of the pressure. I guess I also liked you from the start, too...Just took me a while to realise it. I didn't really know until..." she lifted her head to look at him, "until I thought you were on a date with Jenny. I realised I really didn't like it. At all."

He grinned. "But she and I look so alike."

"I didn't notice, but even if I had - people date people who look like them *all* the time. It's a thing," she said, scooping some more pasta shells into her mouth.

"Well, thankfully not in our case!" he laughed.

"Are you really over Alison?" The words were out before she could stop herself. She had barely known she was going to ask, but it was important she knew the truth.

He nodded slowly and seriously, holding her eyes. "Yes. I've thought long and hard about that. The relationship was terminally broken for a long time before anything happened between her and that guy."

At the mention of Miles, Lyra felt her heart thud. She still hadn't told Alex that Miles had kissed her. She didn't want to ruin the beautiful picnic, the beautiful moment. It wasn't as though Miles meant anything to her, or that there was a real history there. Maybe it was something they could talk about later, when Alison was a very distant memory and they could laugh about it…

"If anything, Alison did us both a favour," Alex continued. "We needed a breaking point, and that ended up being it. I won't pretend it didn't hurt, but the more I thought about it, the more I realised it was pride and not my heart that was hurt."

Lyra nodded and they fell silent. That was closure enough for her. She believed him. It would perhaps be a little odd the next time she saw Alison, but that was a bridge she could cross later. There were a lot of bridges to cross later, she realised. They were beginning to stack up.

Lyra *had* to tell him about Margot. She couldn't keep pretending her phone was broken, or that Silas's number was hers. She drew a deep breath, steeling herself and opened her mouth to begin the strange tale of the non-existent manager.

At that moment, Alex leaned forward and kissed her

tentatively. All thoughts immediately left her mind and there was nothing in the world but the feeling of his lips on hers.

It was like a dam bursting inside. Everything she had been feeling for him, everything she hadn't let herself feel, everything she knew and liked about him came rushing out. She pushed him backwards and they laughed and kissed as she urgently tugged his shirt up and then fumbled with his belt. He moved to kiss her neck and every cell in her body lit on fire with desire. Despite the coolness of the evening, their picnic blanket was being set alight.

"Lyra?" he whispered in her ear, rubbing a hand up her spine and sending waves tingling downward.

"The answer is yes, yes, yes."

CHAPTER THIRTY

Lyra woke early, alone in her own bed, and instantly broke into a huge smile. She stretched joyfully as she thought about last night. Perfect date, perfect evening...perfect guy. She couldn't believe there was ever a time where she hadn't been interested in Alex. Her head felt full of him.

"Alex," she said aloud, savouring the taste of his name in her mouth. She rolled over and squashed her face into the pillow, squealing in childish joy. Then she pulled herself together, remembering that she was a grown woman with a Very Important Meeting today. She and Mick were off to Teller's Music, to either be humiliated when they learned there was no meeting, or to find out what the meeting was about.

Lyra padded downstairs to make coffee and found a despondent Silas sitting at the dining table with his head slumped in his hands.

"Morning?"

He sat bolt upright in alarm, not having heard her enter the room.

"What's the matter?" she asked. He'd already made coffee so she poured some into her favourite old chipped mug and sat opposite him, pulling her knees up to her chin on the chair. The mug made her think of the wine glasses Alex had used last night and she couldn't suppress a huge grin.

Silas glared at her. "Well, no prizes for guessing what you got up to last night."

She blushed, much to her annoyance, and decided to disregard his statement. "Did something happen with Ernie?" she asked, as gently as she could.

"Why would that bother me?" he asked irritably.

She sighed. "Okay, then...did something happen with The Pie-ganic?"

Silas sat still for a moment. He seemed to be weighing something up. Then he said, "I thought I didn't want the ugly pie."

Lyra realised immediately that they weren't talking about pies and that this would be her emotionally-stunted brother's metaphor.

"There was never any ugly pie." Lyra took a sip of the coffee. "But, you know, it's pretty subjective as to what makes an ugly pie. I saw a cute pie."

Silas looked mournfully at her. "That might be the case, but...I'm used to beautiful pies."

Lyra tilted her head at him. "No two people have exactly the same taste. I think he's beautiful."

Silas drew a deep breath and slowly nodded. "He got sick of waiting. And is no longer interested in me."

Lyra's heart sank. Just as Silas had finally realised how interested he was in Ernie, Ernie had thrown in the towel. She put her mug down firmly. "What are you going to do to try and get him back?"

"I don't know."

"Ha. Brother, people have always fallen at your feet, so

you've never had to be creative in the romantic stakes. Ernie's going to need a big gesture. A public declaration. You're basically going to have to make a fool of yourself for him."

"No," Silas said flatly. "No."

"Okay." She sighed and stood. "I have to go get ready for my meeting. Let me know when you want to bounce some ideas around."

She left him sitting there, still in his pyjamas and with bird's nest hair that indicated he hadn't slept a wink.

"It's just up here on the left," Lyra said to the taxi driver as they reached Mick's street. The driver pulled over and honked. Lyra realised she had forgotten to confess Margot to Alex. She couldn't carry on with the charade now. She wanted something more to happen between them, much more, and a secret like this didn't make sense to keep.

On the purely practical side, she wanted to call and text him. She felt sure she could tell the story in a funny way, a way that might make it seem less of a weird lie than it was. She texted Silas to send through Alex's number.

Mick finally came out, after three extra dollars had been rung up on the taxi metre, and just when Lyra was about to get out of the car and burst into his place like the FBI.

"Sorry," he said, slightly out of breath as he slid into the backseat with her. "I got my belt hooked on the back door and couldn't get myself off." Lyra couldn't help but laugh. "Have you figured out what the meeting is about?" Mick asked as the taxi pulled away. She shrugged her shoulders no.

"Best case scenario, it's an actual meeting with an actual record label," she grinned as Mick crossed his fingers, "and worst case scenario, we turn up and no one has any idea who we are or what we're doing there."

Silas, still sulky, texted back telling her she should already have Alex's number, since hadn't he made a call to Margot? Lyra scrolled through her call list for an unsaved number. There it was.

Alex? She texted, wanting to make sure it was him before she bared her soul to a complete stranger. Or worse still, someone she knew.

The text was marked as read just a moment later. *Yes?*

I can't stop thinking about you... she wrote. To her horror it sat unread, remained unread through the short drive during which Mick told Lyra all about how well things were going with Kathryn, and was still unread when they pulled up out the front of the address.

"Cash or card?" the driver asked.

Now that they were really outside the imposing building, it seemed highly unlikely to Lyra that they had actually been invited to a meeting within its walls. She looked at Mick, who was nodding back at her, looking impressed.

"Hello?" the driver said, turning around in concern.

"Sorry, sorry, sorry," she said, gathering herself. "Are you sure this is the place?"

"Been driving cabs in this town for twenty-six years," he said irritably, "so, yeah."

Lyra and Mick exchanged another look before they paid the driver and got out. They took a moment to dance a tiny little jig with one another, right there in the street - arms hooked at the elbow and going around in a circle.

CHAPTER THIRTY-ONE

A s they entered the building through the grand double doors, Mick stumbled slightly on the corner of the oversized vintage rug filling the foyer.

"Please, try to play it cool," Lyra said to him under her breath.

"Are you talking to me or yourself?" he asked and she grinned.

The studio reeked of cool and they looked around in awe. The entrance was filled with odd, old furniture, much of which looked like the kind of stuff Lyra's grandmother had had in her place, but probably cost more per piece than she'd earned her entire life. Huge framed posters of Tellers' biggest signed acts hung from the walls, their frames gilded as though in a museum. For one crazy moment, Lyra let herself picture how she and Mick would look up there. The lightning scar had to be on show, she decided.

A ridiculously attractive young man in a mesh tank top that showed off his muscles sneered at them as they approached his DJ table-reception desk. Diamante-encrusted headphones dangled around his neck.

"Aloha?" he said, in a manner that suggested he had much better things to be doing.

"Lyra and Mick. We have a meeting at 11." Lyra tried to keep the questioning note out of her voice.

He nodded as if they were boring him with details he already knew. At that moment, a door appeared in the wall of books behind the receptionist. A beautiful woman in her mid-fifties, with a stylish silver-grey bob and huge pearl earrings peeped her head out. Lyra immediately recognised Selena Teller, owner of the label. She was star-struck.

"Oh great, you're here," Selena said warmly and instantly the receptionist's attitude changed.

"I was just about to show them in, Selena," he said sweetly. "Can I get you guys something to drink?" He turned back to them with a radiant smile. "Champagne? Whiskey?"

"Nothing for me, thanks," Mick said, heading confidently toward Selena.

"Water, please." Lyra tried to keep her voice steady.

Selena met them halfway. "I'll take them in, Todd, you bring the water." She gave Lyra the briefest of hugs, which smelled of subtle and expensive perfume, and did the same with Mick. "We're excited to meet you," she said. "Follow me."

Lyra wondered whether she was actually dreaming the entire thing. Or hallucinating. She leaned forward and gently pinched Mick; he swatted her away.

As Selena led them down a plush carpeted corridor, Lyra's phone pinged. A message from Alex. She quickly and eagerly opened it.

I'd like to keep it professional. I'm seeing someone.

Her heart pounded, before she realised he thought she was Margot. *Seeing someone.* The words made her glow.

Selena led them into a meeting room where two other executives were already sitting. There was Elsa, wearing a silk fuchsia blouse, her hair neatly braided, and Steve, a middle-aged man wearing almost comically large, thick-rimmed glasses. As they shook hands, a third figure in a high-backed swivel chair spun to face them and Lyra's jaw dropped. It was Alex.

"Surprise!" he said. Selena, Elsa and Steve smiled.

"*What?*" Lyra was glad she was sitting down, otherwise she may have fallen. "What are *you* doing here?"

Alex grinned, his eyes holding hers. Lyra's heart set off on a wild rhythm, and she felt heat colour her cheeks. She gratefully took a sip of the water Todd brought in at that moment.

"I called in a few favours to get you this meeting," Alex said and Steve laughed.

"More like all the favours ever," Steve said, then turned to Lyra to explain. "Alex went to uni with my son Liam. Liam has dyslexia and Alex tutored him basically the whole way through, and helped us get a diagnosis and then the support he needed. Liam is only where he is now because of Alex."

Lyra felt her heart swell with pride. She beamed at Alex who looked slightly abashed at the praise.

"Okay, let's get started, shall we?" Selena asked. "Does anyone know what time Margot will be getting here?" Lyra froze in horror, the inklings of a nightmare beginning to stir. "Will she be much longer?" There was a note of impatience creeping into her voice. This was a woman unaccustomed to being kept waiting.

"She, uh, she...Margot couldn't," Lyra swallowed hard, feeling all eyes in the room trained on her. "She couldn't... could she, Mick?" She turned to him desperately. He opened and closed his mouth, eyes widening.

"She was in an accident and got struck by lightning," Mick blurted, then lost his way. "She's...she was rushed to hospital. It's very serious, they're not sure when...she'll be conscious again." Lyra assumed it was the first story that occurred to poor Mick, given his history.

Three of the four faces around them registered shock. Elsa's hand flew to her heart. Only Selena seemed unmoved. Her eyes had narrowed and she looked back and forth between Lyra and Mick. Lyra didn't blame her. Mick wasn't going to win any Academy Awards for that performance. And Lyra felt like the worst person in the world, having completely thrown him under a bus.

"I got a text from her just a few minutes ago?" Alex said finally, sounding confused.

"There must be a misunderstanding then," Selena said coldly. Lyra couldn't bring herself to meet her gaze. She had never wished so fervently for the floor to open up and swallow her. Whole. For eternity. Her eyes were glued to the table and her face was aflame.

"What did the text say?" Elsa asked hopefully, as Alex pulled out his phone. She leaned over before he could react.

"I can't stop thinking about you..." Elsa read, trailing off. She looked at Selena.

Alex was helpless. "No, no, no, it's not what it sounds like!"

"Alex, are you sleeping with their manager? Is that the only reason you asked for this meeting?" Selena's voice was brisk.

Lyra wanted to jump to Alex's defence and confess the whole stupid situation but her tongue was glued silent inside her mouth. She could only look mournfully at him and then back down at the table.

Steve piped up, looking mortified. "No - he, Alex, he played me their demo. Selena, they're really very good. *Very* good."

"Good perhaps, but not professional. Call Margot please, Alex," Selena said.

Lyra could feel Alex's eyes on her and she forced herself to meet them. She felt tears welling. There was heat radiating from Selena and a desperate, silent plea from Steve.

"On loudspeaker," Selena added firmly, in a tone that brooked no refusal.

Too late, Lyra realised what would happen and made a lame grab for her handbag. Everyone in the room sat silently as the phone inside it rang loud, clear and incriminating for what felt to Lyra like an eternity.

Alex hung up, frowning, and her phone stopped ringing. There was a vacuum of quiet in the room. Then Lyra drew a deep breath and raised her head. She had to at least try and explain. For Mick's sake. For Alex's sake. For Steve's sake.

"We weren't getting booked," she said quietly. "Everyone kept asking for a manager and I didn't know how to get us one or if we could afford it. It seemed like a good idea to..." she drew a deep breath. "To invent-"

"I made her do it," Mick said suddenly and firmly, looking around the room with his chin jutting forward. "I invented Margot, I added her to our posters, I convinced Lyra to lie. It was all my idea, don't you blame her. She's trying to take the fall for me. I'm going to step out here, but you should continue this meeting." He turned to face Selena. She was stony, but had raised an eyebrow. "You should meet with this young woman because she is talented and passionate and loyal, and you have no idea what she's overcome. She sings like an angel and she writes like Shakespeare, and you'd be doing yourself and your label a great disservice if you ended this here."

At his words, the tears escaped Lyra and Elsa quietly nudged a tissue box towards her.

Selena clenched and unclenched her jaw. "We have a lot of talent on our books," she said finally. "For the most part, they are wonderful *adults* who require no supervision and do nothing to bring the label into disrepute." She raised her water glass with an unhurried motion and took a long sip. She set it down carefully and folded her hands on the table. "And then, there are a few that give us constant trouble. They're in the minority, but it doesn't feel that way. We often have to get our PR teams to clean up their messes after them. We need to leverage our goodwill with the media to keep them out of the spotlight. We have to make unsavoury partnerships to preserve their good image. And we have to treat them like children, monitoring their social media and their evenings out. These people are costly and unreliable. And a stunt like this is exactly the kind of thing they'd pull."

There was a moment of silence and Lyra studied her hands. Mick stood up to leave.

"Wait," Selena said, holding up a hand. Mick froze halfway out of his seat. Lyra felt everyone in the room hold their breath. "Take her out of here with you, please."

As they walked back out through the foyer, Todd smirked at them. Lyra texted the girls that she needed an emergency meeting at the Whistle Stop, as soon as they could get there.

By the time Marley and Amy arrived, Lyra was two drinks in. Mick had offered to join her, but she felt horrible for having dragged him through the meeting at Teller's. She wanted him to have the space to be angry at her and wanted to cry without him feeling guilty. Eliza had served Lyra her drinks and hadn't asked a word about her blotchy, tear-stained face. It had almost seemed to please her.

Amy and Marley strode in, concern etched in their faces. They wrapped Lyra tightly in hugs and she tried not to break down. Once they had drinks, the three of them fell into silence. Amy gently laid a hand on Lyra's arm and Marley bit the side of her mouth.

"I feel completely responsible," Amy said sadly. "Margot was all my idea."

Lyra shook her head and blew her nose, the loud noise turning some heads. She didn't care.

"It's not your fault, Amy," Marley said, downcast. "It's mine. If I hadn't been so drunk when I took down the message, I would have remembered that both Lyra *and* Margot were supposed to show."

"You guys are sweet." Lyra smiled a little. "But no. I did it. I should have told Alex sooner. I should have told him right at the start. I just...never found the proper moment."

"Well, you didn't know he'd do something like this," Marley said. "Something so beautiful and so incredibly supportive."

Lyra felt Amy gently nudge Marley with her foot as Lyra's tears welled fresh again. "She's right though," Lyra said to Amy. "It's so supportive. And I made a giant idiot of him and that Steve guy, and myself, not to mention poor Mick, in front of the head of a record label. Oh my God." She dropped her head into her hands.

"Well," Amy said, after stroking her hair after a moment, "it's not the only record label in town. And you still have your voice, you still have Mick."

"He was so good about it," she said mournfully.

"You still have Si and the truck," Amy continued, nodding. "And you'll *always* have us."

"Thank you," she whispered. "Ugh. Thanks for listening to me." She wiped her face and blew her nose again, trying to get her emotions under control.

Amy shook her head. "It's going to take a while to get over it. We're here. Keep crying if you want, keep talking about it. There's no rush...Have you tried calling Alex?" she asked gently.

"More times than my pride allowed. He won't pick up."

Miles walked into the bar and spotted Lyra, frowning as he took in her face. As Eliza watched from near the bar, he came over to their table and touched Lyra's shoulder in concern. "Hey. I haven't seen you for ages. Are you okay?"

She shrunk from him. All she wanted now was Alex. She realised she'd never seriously been interested in Miles, nor he in her. Too bad it was only crystal clear now that it was too late.

"She had some bad news, but she's fine," Amy said.

"You could get us some drinks," Marley added and Miles glared at her before smiling blandly.

"I'm not actually working, but okay. What will it be?"

Amy ordered and Miles walked away.

"How's work?" Lyra asked her, desperately needing a distraction.

Amy shrugged. "I think they're considering downsizing."

"They won't get rid of you, though," Marley said with certainty. "You're amazing."

"Downsizing is downsizing. I've got seniority and I make our boss good money, but so do others."

"Sorry that you're feeling insecure, Amy," Lyra said. "I'm sure you could get a job anywhere in this town, but it's not a nice feeling. There's a backup job in The Pie-ganic if ever you need one, which I'm sure you won't."

Amy smiled and her thoughts turned faraway for a second. Lyra and Marley shared a look.

"Have you spoken to Rick yet?" Lyra asked Amy gently.

Amy shook her head and then snapped herself back to the present. "There is no 'yet'. It's over."

Lyra nodded.

"Lena?" An incredulous voice spoke from behind them. "Lena, is that really you?"

Lyra turned to see a woman gawping at Marley, her mouth a wide O of disbelief. It seemed to take Marley a moment to realise the woman was talking to her. Then she shrugged and shook her head, looking at the girls, then back at the woman.

"No?" she said, sounding slightly bewildered.

The woman continued to stare at her. "It is you. It is! I'd recognise you anywhere."

Amy frowned. "This is *Marley*," she said firmly. "She might look like your Lena, but this isn't her. Sorry for your misunderstanding."

The woman stood for another long moment, staring hard at Marley. Then she shook herself out of it and mumbled an apology before finally turning. She took several glances back at Marley as she left the bar.

From the corner of her eye, Lyra thought she saw Marley mouth a "thank you" to Amy but when Lyra looked up, Marley's face was calm but confused. "Well, that was weird," she laughed. "Apparently I have a doppelganger!"

"I wish I had one," Lyra said. "I wish my doppelganger had made all that trouble for me today. My God, is there a bigger idiot in the world than me?" Fresh tears welled, just as Miles returned with their drinks. He squeezed her shoulder.

"These are on the house." He lingered for a moment and Marley seemed to sense Lyra's annoyance.

"Someone over there's trying to get your attention," she said, gesturing vaguely towards the opposite corner of the bar.

Miles squinted in that direction. "I don't see anyone and I need to head back home."

"I do," Amy said pointedly. "Right over there."

Miles got the hint and dropped his hand from Lyra's

shoulder, looking irritated. "I'll message you, Lyra," he said, as he walked away. She didn't respond.

An hour later, all Lyra wanted was to be under the covers of her bed, blocking out the world.

"Guys, I'm so sorry," she said, being struck all over again by everything that had happened that day. "I think I just need to go home and wallow."

They nodded in sympathy. "Of course." Amy kissed her on the cheek and gave her a huge hug. "Shall we walk you home?"

She shook her head. "Thank you, though. I'll call you tomorrow."

"Goodnight," Marley said as they hugged. "Can you text us when you get home?"

Lyra nodded, grabbing her jacket and heading off, hoping the evening air and a walk would help get her thoughts under control.

She hadn't gone far when her phone rang. She pulled it eagerly from her bag, hoping it was Alex. It was Miles. She hung up and he immediately rang again, then twice more. Concerned it might have something to do with Marley or Amy, Lyra finally picked up.

"What is it?"

"Listen, I know you're not my biggest fan right now, with the way things turned out between us-"

"That's not-" she began, but realised she didn't have the energy to argue.

"But I've been thinking. You've still never gigged at the bar. You never got your manager to call me, and we have a spare spot next Saturday."

"I don't have a manager," she said flatly. "I never had one. I lied about it. Okay?" She went to hang up.

"Lyra, wait! Listen, that's perfect actually. Maybe I can change that. I really think I might be able to help you get a manager. The gig will pay decent money and it's a really good chance for someone starting out. I want to give you that chance. But you'd need to meet me tonight."

Lyra paused. Could this be a way to make things up to Mick? To get another shot, this time with a proper, actual manager? She sighed. "I'm tired, Miles. I just want to go home."

"Please," he said. "I can really help you out here. No effort on your part. My flat is close by. You don't have to do a thing, just come over and hear me out." He sensed her hesitation. "Ten minutes. Give me ten minutes and if you don't like what you hear, you can leave."

CHAPTER THIRTY-TWO

"**L**et me take your jacket," Miles said. His flat was small, filled with records and art posters - mostly nude women - and lit in a flattering, warm way. There wasn't much furniture in the living room, just a bar corner and a soft, oversized sofa. The kind of sofa that made Lyra want to curl up and fall asleep on.

"Do you know Eliza's standing outside?" Lyra asked uncertainly. The other woman had frightened her when she'd buzzed up to Miles' apartment.

"Oh yeah," he chuckled. "She does that sometimes."

"And...you're okay with that?" She handed him her jacket, frowning.

He shrugged. "I'm not making her do it."

"But isn't she supposed to be at work right now?"

"She's finished. I was just in to check the roster, because I couldn't get through on the phone. Can I get you a drink?"

"Just water." Lyra realised that was all the explanation she was going to get on the Eliza topic. "I'm not going to stay long."

He nodded. "Okay, let me fix myself a proper drink first

and then we can talk." He gestured to his record player. "Put on whatever record you like."

Lyra scoured the shelves for a familiar band name, artist name...anything she'd ever heard of before. But every time she slid a thin record out from the packed shelves, the name was incomprehensible. She didn't exactly listen to top forty music, either. She felt Miles watching her from across the room and realised he probably used this trick often - creating an opportunity to judge women by the number of obscure names they knew. Lyra didn't have the energy to care. Almost all the records were from solo male artists, which Lyra found odd considering he only booked women to play at the Whistle Stop. Finally, she saw a name she recognised and slipped the record from its cover, gently dropping the needle just as Miles finished mixing his drink.

"Nice," he said, nodding in approval and coming over to the sofa with his drink and water for her. "Chesko Shadelfrod. He's doing amazing stuff over there on the West Side."

"Perth?" Lyra asked, having heard Chesko's name but not being familiar with his entire backstory.

Miles laughed. "No, Chicago." She was mildly embarrassed, but shrugged it off. "Okay, so real talk," Miles said. He sat down a little too close to Lyra. She scooted backward ever so slightly, and he noticed. He waited for a beat. "There's been a cancellation for next Saturday night at the bar." She nodded slowly. "And, the thing is I'd really love to give you that spot. As you know, the Whistle Stop is a great venue, some of the acts have gone on to have much bigger gigs after playing there."

Lyra had to assume it was true, but it seemed unlikely. Talent scouts were hardly hanging out at the Whistle Stop, were they? Perhaps they were, she didn't know the first thing about them.

"Okay, great. That sounds good. Thanks. You mentioned

something about a manager?"

"That's what I meant. It would be great exposure, and it could help you get a manager. But it's not guaranteed yet. There are two people that we're looking at for the gig at the moment."

"Right," she said flatly.

"I mean, I *want* it to be you. But I guess it kind of depends..." He let his voice trail off. The air became thick with tension.

"Depends on what?"

She thought of all the acts Miles had booked to play at the Whistle Stop. There wasn't a type, per se, but there was one thing they all had in common. They were beautiful. And they were women. Had they also sat here, on this sofa? And what had they done? Made deals with Miles? She had to know exactly what he meant. She would force him to admit it.

"I guess it depends on our friendship," Miles said finally, his face open and friendly.

"So say we're friends." Lyra picked up her water and took a sip, holding his gaze the whole time. "Then what?"

He smiled at her, and moved slightly closer again. She froze. She didn't feel endangered, just annoyed. Miles was an opportunistic creep, but that seemed to be the extent of it.

"What kind of friends are we exactly, Lyra?"

"The kind of friends who get each other gigs and help each other out if they can?" she said, surprised he wasn't picking up her disinterest.

Miles nodded slowly. "Yes, I guess we are that kind of friends."

His phone beeped as a message came in. He didn't even try to disguise the fact that he was eager to check it. He immediately picked it up and flicked his finger over the screen to open the message. Lyra sat still, drinking her water. Whatever he saw on the screen made him grin.

"Funny joke?" she guessed out loud.

"Huh?" He looked up from his screen as if he had completely forgotten she was there. "Oh, no. It's uh...an old friend. She might be stopping around soon."

"Okay, well, I guess I'd best be off." She set down her water glass and stood. Miles nodded, phone still held firmly in his hand. He made a half-hearted show of getting up. "Please," she said, holding up her hand, "I can see myself out." As she reached the door, she turned back to him, his face illuminated in the greenish glow of his cell. "So, you'll let me know about the gig, right?"

"Yeah, yeah, sure," he said, smiling. "I'll get back to you."

She let herself out and walked down the hall to the apartment staircase, shaking her head. She hoped no one would fall for his tricks, although he was playing them half-heartedly. It was as though he knew that with his good looks, he really didn't have to try that hard to dupe anyone. If one woman passed on his game, the next would be along right away. Lyra pitied poor, besotted Eliza.

As she was heading down the stairs, she crossed paths with a beautiful young woman in skin-tight wet-look leggings and a sequined top. Her thick blonde hair was held up in a perfectly messy bun and as they passed one another, Lyra noticed an arm full of tattoos portraying musical instruments.

Lyra bit her lip, but was unable to stay quiet. "Excuse me?" The woman turned around, and smiled in a friendly and expectant way. "He's not worth it, you know."

The woman paused for a moment and it was clear she knew exactly what Lyra meant. Finally she shrugged. "He's fun. And I don't really care about anything else."

And she waggled her fingers as a farewell, then turned and walked off.

❖

As Lyra walked out of the apartment block, still shaking her head, she ran directly into someone.

"Sorry," she said reflexively, sticking out her arms to steady herself. She looked up and her heart stopped.

"*Lyra?*" Alex said, stunned. He was with a male friend, who Lyra realised must have known who she was, since he looked at the ground in mild embarrassment once he heard her name.

"Oh, Alex, I'm *so* happy to see you!" She didn't care about dignity, just wanted to make things right between them, whatever that took. "You have no idea how happy. I can explain what happened today. Please, you have to listen to me and hear me out. It will all make sense."

Suddenly a window opened on the second floor of the apartment building and Miles called out. "Hey, Lyra," he yelled and Alex looked up. When he spotted Miles, his jaw clenched tightly as shock rippled through his body. "Lyra, you forgot your jacket." Miles let it drift down from the window and onto the street, closing the window behind him.

Alex was stock still and Lyra was flooded with desperate panic. "Nonono," she said quickly, stepping towards him. "No, that is *not* what it looks like." He took a huge step back from her, his eyes hurt and angry. "Alex, *please,*" she begged. "Nothing has *ever* happened with Miles-"

"But you know who he is?" Alex began, in a low, tense voice. Lyra felt a chill at the sound of it. "You *know* who he is and you didn't say anything even though I told you all about what happened with Alison."

"Yes," she stammered, "yes, I do know who he is and I should have told you that I knew him. I realise that now, I have no excuse for that. But you need to believe me, he is *nothing* to me and never has been."

"That's a lie, she kissed him," a voice said. Eliza stepped out of the shadows, her arms crossed over her chest and her face pinched and bitter.

"Okay, you are *completely* unstable," Lyra said, clutching her hand to her heart.

"Is that true?" Alex demanded, looking horrified. His voice was thick with emotion. "Oh my God, Lyra, is that true? Tell me *honestly.*"

She bit her lip, tears welling in her eyes. She didn't want to let them out. Didn't want him to think she was being manipulative. Another lie now would make things an even bigger mess, but the truth would push him away from her. Maybe forever.

"It's true but it's not the truth."

"What the hell does that mean?" Alex demanded, half-laughing in exasperation.

"It means yes we kissed, but I don't like him. I never liked him. He kissed me, he asked me to come here tonight-"

"And you did?" Alex asked, in cold disbelief. "After last night you just couldn't wait to jump into someone else's arms?"

"No," she shook her head vigorously, but couldn't stop the tears now. They flowed freely down her face. "Alex, *please* listen to me, it's not like that at all!"

"It's been a weird day," Alex snapped, cutting her off. "I have a lot to think about. I guess we both do. I want to make sure you get home safe, okay? I'm going to flag down a taxi. I don't know if you have money on you, so here's a fifty."

"Alex, you don't understand-"

She tried to grab his hand but he pulled it away and stepped out onto the street, waving at an oncoming cab. Lyra looked pleadingly at his friend, who looked away quickly and studied the pavement.

"Lyra," Alex said stiffly, "I *don't* want to talk to you now."

The taxi pulled up and he opened the door and leaned in, giving the driver her address.

"No," she said, shaking her head. "I'm not getting in until you listen to me." Her nose was running and she was sure there was makeup all over her face, but she didn't care.

"Please, Lyra." He sounded so tired that she couldn't bear it.

"I'm only getting in because I do care about you," she sobbed, "I care about you so much and I don't know how this day went so wrong and it's all my fault." She put one leg into the taxi, reluctantly. "But you have to know how much I care." She looked pleadingly at his stony face. His eyes were downcast and his shoulders slumped. He wouldn't meet her eye. She got in and he shut the door gently behind her. The driver pulled away quickly and the last thing Lyra saw was Eliza, smirking.

Her phone pinged and she frantically tried to unlock the screen, hoping it was a message from Alex telling her to stop, to turn the cab around. It was from Miles: *I think we're going to go in a different direction with the gig. Sorry.*

She switched off the phone. At least Miles was predictable. And at least she knew beyond all doubt that she didn't care about him.

Alex was a different story and she had blown it. The thought of him made her heart ache. She leaned back and pictured his grey-gold eyes and the little scar under his lip. She thought of him with Murgatroyd, with the shy teenage boy, on the beach dressed up for the wedding, at the hospital, on the picnic blanket beside the runway....

There was no way to win him back now, she knew that. He was lost to her forever and she'd never feel those strong arms around her again. Never get to taste another of his kisses. To the driver's great embarrassment and her own, she burst into fresh, loud and inconsolable tears.

CHAPTER THIRTY-THREE

When the taxi pulled up outside her place, Lyra shoved the fifty dollar note Alex had given her at the delighted driver and quickly got out. She hoped Silas was home, she needed a drink and a hug. He might tease her and tell her it was her fault, but she knew he'd give her the comfort she needed.

"Hello?" she called, shutting the front door and kicking off her shoes. She slid her feet into her slippers. Silas's jacket was hanging up so she knew he was home.

"In the kitchen," came the reply. His voice sounded muffled.

She frowned and walked quickly towards the voice. Silas was sitting at the kitchen table hugging his knees, surrounded by balled up tissues and two empty wine bottles.

"Oh *no*," Lyra said, as he looked up at her with red-rimmed eyes. She saw from the shock in his face how bad she looked too.

"What happened to you?" he asked.

Lyra had never seen her brother like this. Not even once. Whatever she was going through, it would have to wait.

"Nothing at all," she said, shaking her head. "Is there any wine left?"

He lifted a third bottle from his lap. It was three quarters full. She grabbed a glass and sat down, taking the bottle from him and pouring herself a generous slug. She gulped it down, poured another and then put her glass on the table, folded her arms and looked at him. "Spare me no details."

He nodded. "Mick and Mum had an affair," he said bluntly.

"What?" She laughed, shocked. "No they didn't." But as the words came out, she realised that might not be true. The tension between Mick and Silas, Silas warning her that their mum wasn't perfect, Mick's philosophical attitude about being cheated on by his wife. Those things would all make sense if... "What the *hell*?"

Silas nodded. "Yep."

They sat there staring at each other for a long moment, Lyra's mouth hanging open. Then she rubbed her temples, squeezing her eyes shut. "What, when, how..." she shook her head in bewilderment, "and how did you find out?"

"I had suspicions. I always had suspicions."

"Did you?" she asked, incredulous. "I didn't. I could literally not be more surprised. And a *lot* has surprised me today."

"You were younger than me," Silas said. "But anyway, I never really thought anything of it. If anything, I thought Dad would deserve it if it was true."

She nodded slowly. "But how did you find out for sure?"

"I found a love letter."

"Where the hell did you find a love letter?"

"It was in a book. In one of the armfuls I managed to rescue from Mum's bookshelf before the wicked witch" - their stepmother - "threw them all out. I think you were at a sleepover that day."

"I remember it though. I guess you told me when I got back?"

He nodded. "I've never really looked through the books, but I've kept them this whole time, through all our moves. There was one about the magic of crystals."

They both smiled at that. Their mother had been a huge crystal lover, believing strongly in their healing powers.

"It was inside that one?" Silas nodded. "Why were you looking at crystal healing?"

He shrugged. "I just felt drawn to it one day. I was thinking about her and I realised I'd never looked through them. That one stood out to me. And then, when I found the letter, I confronted Mick."

Lyra took a long sip of the wine and got up to put some bread in the toaster for Silas. He didn't look as though he'd eaten and he was going to have one hell of a hangover if he didn't digest something to sop up the alcohol.

"What did Mick say?" She paused to quickly examine how she felt about Mick on hearing this news. She wasn't mad at him, she knew that much. She was definitely surprised, but the more she thought about it, the more it made sense. She had memories of Mick and Mum making each other laugh. She didn't have any memories like that of her mum and dad.

"He seemed relieved," Silas said. "She'd made him promise never to tell us, especially after she found out she was going to die."

Lyra nodded, turning away from Silas to look down at the toaster, forcing her tears back. She swallowed hard and studied the glowing filament in the toaster.

"Okay," she said finally, her voice unsteady.

"But then," Silas stopped to blow his nose, "but then I asked if our father knew."

The toast popped up and Lyra slicked butter onto it and placed it on a dish in front of Silas. "Did he?"

Silas's eyes welled again and Lyra knew they'd arrived at the sticking point. "Dad found out the night he had the accident. That's why he was drunk driving. Apparently, he didn't usually drink and drive and, honestly, I can't remember a time that he did that, aside from that night. But he wanted to get away from Mick after he found out."

"Oh." Silas looked mournfully at her.

"Lyra, if Mick hadn't had the affair, Dad wouldn't have driven drunk and then he wouldn't have been in AA and he wouldn't have met that...*woman.*" He couldn't stop the tears from spilling over then and choked back a sob.

Lyra's heart broke. Silas imagined a different life for them, one where they still lived with their father. One where Silas hadn't been sent away to a conversion therapy camp, one where he hadn't come home to find his belonging strewn on the lawn like garbage and the locks changed. Lyra hadn't realised how much pain Silas was still in. Her poor, poor beautiful brother. If only the life he imagined were possible.

She dragged her chair around the table and put it next to his, slipping her arm around his shoulders and pulling him to her. He leaned against her, his body shaking with tears as she stroked his hair.

"Silas," she said gently after a while, "maybe you don't want to hear this, but Dad needed to be in AA. He was sick. Remember the first step? He was powerless over alcohol and his life had become unmanageable. And honestly... She didn't make him do those things. We're *his* kids, not hers. He should have stood up for us. He should be standing up for us now. I know we have some good memories of our childhood with him, and I know he's not all bad. But if you let someone come between you and your children, you *do not deserve those children.*" Lyra's voice shook with anger as she said those last words.

After a long moment she could feel Silas nodding. He

slowly pulled himself up from her and wiped his eyes, looking at her sadly.

"You're so right, Ly. You're so right. He doesn't deserve us."

She nodded. "You know who has been with us through it all?"

"Mick," he said sadly.

"And if Mum loved him…"

Silas nodded slowly. "Ugh, I hate how right you are." He ran a clean tissue over his face, blowing his nose and wiping his eyes.

"You have no idea how badly I messed up every single thing I had going for me today," she said. "At least I can be right about one thing."

CHAPTER THIRTY-FOUR

On their mother's anniversary, the wind was whipping through the trees at the cemetery. Beyond, the ocean was choppy and grey. Lyra had always thought their mother had picked a perfect resting place for herself and liked to think she could feel the sea air, wherever she was.

She and Silas were dressed as colourfully as they could manage - more difficult for Silas than for Lyra. Their mother had always hated black.

Lyra was feeling surprisingly steady this anniversary. Previous ones had felt much more difficult and she'd usually woken feeling heavy and broken. But since she'd learned about her mother and Mick, it had felt as though she'd been given a gift.

Someone else who'd been close to their mother, that she had loved and who had loved her, who was old enough to have proper memories and stories of her. Lyra felt as though she could get to know her mother better. And knowing she made mistakes, just like Lyra did - like Lyra didn't seem to be able to stop doing - it made her more forgiving of herself.

Lyra knew Mick and Kathryn, Alex's aunt, were becoming closer, so she had hesitated to ask Mick to talk to her about her mother. But his whole face had lit up when she had mentioned her. He had many stories to share and he was eager to share them - stories about how they'd slowly started falling in love, how they'd felt almost powerless to stop what was happening between them, how she'd refused to leave their father and break up the family.

That last part had felt particularly upsetting - the family would end up more broken than she could ever have imagined. Maybe if she'd gotten together with Mick, it would have remained a little more intact. But she couldn't have seen the future.

"Did you bring her hot chocolate?" Silas asked, rooting through his satchel. "I can't find the flask, I've only got mine."

"It's here." Lyra pulled it from the side pocket of her backpack. They'd started a ritual many years ago of making hot chocolate to her recipe and bringing three flasks. They would drink theirs and, as they chatted to her, they'd slowly pour hers into the earth.

They spread out a blanket now and sat down, hugging their jackets around themselves. Lyra felt grateful it wasn't raining, but the wind was biting. Her cheeks stung and her nose was red from cold.

"Hi, Mummy," she said, settling in. "Lovely weather we're having."

"Wait till you hear the mess Lyra's gotten herself into." Silas sat down beside her and slung an arm over her shoulders. "She invented a fictional band manager, got caught out on the lie during a meeting with a record label, which screwed over the guy who got her the meeting in the first place, who she likes by the way, then got caught leaving a *different* guy's apartment-"

"Nothing happened!" Lyra glared at Silas.

"And then lied about it and *then* got caught out in the lie."

Tears sprang to her eyes, blurring her vision. "That's not the whole story," she said, tucking her hair behind her ears against the wind and struggling to suppress a sob.

Silas hugged her close. "Sorry," he said, sounding genuine. "I'm trying to make light of it all…"

Lyra had not had contact with Alex and did not expect to have any now. Her text messages remained unread days after being sent and a letter she had worked up the nerve to give Jenny had been returned unopened. Lyra knew that as far as he was concerned, it was over. But it was hard for her to move on when she thought about him every day and cried about what had happened just as often.

She leaned into Silas to let him know it was okay, then took the lid off her flask and her mother's.

"Oh," she said casually, "and *Silas* met a guy who was totally in love with him, Silas didn't think he was good enough, and when he *finally* realised he was, it was too late and the guy was gone."

"So basically, you raised two pretty hopeless children with no romantic prospects," Silas added. Lyra laughed through her tears and they clinked their cups together, then clinked against hers as a toast.

"Not *completely* hopeless," said a voice behind them. It was Mick. Silas turned in alarm and surprise, but Lyra sprang up and hugged him tightly. She wasn't sure how Silas would react - she hadn't told him that she'd invited Mick along to this anniversary observation.

Silas got stiffly to his feet and the two men stood looking at each other for a long moment. Lyra wasn't sure whether Silas was going to hit him or hug him. Mick looked as though he was ready to accept either one, standing stock still against the wind, his eyes locked on Silas's, not moving.

Then Silas moved forward and threw his arms around

Mick, who stumbled back a step then grabbed onto Silas tightly, returning the hug. There were tears in Mick's eyes and he hugged Silas like he wasn't going to let go. They stayed that way for a long moment, until they started slapping one another's backs. They wiped their eyes and then pretended nothing at all had happened. And that was it.

Lyra had secretly made a fourth flask of hot chocolate for Mick and she pulled it out of her backpack now. As she handed it to him, she explained the ritual. The three of them sat at the grave, talking amongst themselves, and to her, until long after the sun had sunk behind the treeline and the weather had turned absolutely bitter.

It was the best anniversary Lyra could remember and she loved that they'd made a new ritual and widened the circle of love around her mother. Her beautiful, flawed, perfect mother.

CHAPTER THIRTY-FIVE

They plodded slowly out of winter and into spring. Lyra was glad when they no longer woke in complete darkness and she had stopped wearing her thickest coat.

People were more and more frequently taking their boats out on the harbour and the foot traffic was starting to increase again.

She just hadn't been able to forget Alex.

Now that the weather was improving, she would occasionally wander through the Secret Garden and notice which plants were coming to life. She didn't do it often - it made her miss Alex too much. She'd remember snippets of their conversations, or picture him at a table where they'd eaten lunch, or remember his observations about a particular piece of art within the garden. Then everything would sting as freshly as it had that night.

Lyra looked out over Lilac Bay at the jacarandas. Soon they'd bloom, their delicate flowers contrasting brightly against the green and blue. She let Silas serve the next customer.

Silas handed the woman her order - a questionable combination of liver pie with a side of caramelised onions - and slumped back against the drinks fridge. They sighed simultaneously.

"We have *got* to pull ourselves together," Silas said. Lyra nodded but didn't move.

Silas and Ernie hadn't reconciled and neither had Amy and Rick. It seemed to Lyra that winter had broken everyone apart from the ones they loved. At least Lyra had the honour of knowing she had ruined her relationship with Alex in the most spectacular way of all three of them.

Now and again, Lyra thought she caught glimpses of Alex along the promenade. The back of a head disappearing around a corner, the edge of a shoulder leaning out of a doorway. She knew it couldn't be true. Jenny was running Meat is Murder, but usually only opened it a couple of days a week. Judging by her tight smile and curt wave, she knew exactly what had transpired. Even Cameron, the teenager Alex had befriended and who worked with Jenny now and again, didn't make much of an effort with Lyra. The two trucks just worked alongside one another - no mingling.

There was a bright spot in all of this for Lyra, though. All the emotions swirling around her brain and body, everything she'd been trying to get a handle on and process about Alex, had crystallised into song. She finally felt unblocked and the words and creativity were flowing. Tears, grief, confusion, the thwarted beginnings of what might have been love, they had all helped birth a new song. It was a way to try and process what she had lost, before she truly had it. It was an explanation, an ode, a tribute. And Lyra was happy with it. More than happy, she thought it was the best thing she'd ever written. It was a strange thing to say, but the song gave her goosebumps. She'd caught Silas singing it and he hadn't even pretended he'd heard it elsewhere.

"It's good, Lyra," he'd said. "Really, really good."

She knew nothing would happen with the song. Not now that she'd blown her chance with the record label and Selena Teller had probably black-listed her with every producer in the country. Lyra knew she and Mick would play the song in their sets, to whatever disinterested crowd they played next, in whatever dim venue, and that was all the life it would live. But it had opened something in her, and taken her skills to a new level - she could feel that. She had tapped into something new. And once she'd written that song, others had poured from her. The drought was well and truly over. Lyra thought of all the songs she wrote as her children, but she was particularly proud of this first new one: her favourite, her song of lost love.

CHAPTER THIRTY-SIX

S ilas returned from a bathroom break one day the following week and jerked Lyra out of a daydream with a fierce slap to the counter top. Lyra was surprised it didn't crack the glass. She looked at him in shock.

"Look!" he said. "This is it!" He removed his hand and pushed a flyer toward her.

"Lilac Bay Food Truck Fridays," she read. "Live music, incredible food and a drinks cart every Friday at six on the promenade." She put the flyer back down on the counter and shrugged. Silas was looking at her expectantly. "That sounds good for business," she said flatly, knowing full well she should be much more excited than she was.

"Read the next line," he urged, slipping the flyer back into her hand. She squinted.

"Musicians and bands sought. Call Juniper." A number was listed. She sighed. "Silas, I'm not going to sing here."

"Why not?"

"I..." She didn't have a good answer, aside from the fact that everything felt like a bridge too far at the moment.

While her writing was flowing, she didn't have much energy for gigs. This suited Mick, enamoured as he was with Kathryn. Their jam sessions had become almost a rarity, as had any social life. She saw the girls once a week or so, although she was avoiding the Whistle Stop, and often did nothing but have a bath or go to bed once she and Silas got home.

"Listen to me," Silas said, getting right into her face. "You told me to make a grand gesture to try and win back Ernie, right?"

She raised an eyebrow at him. "And did you take my advice?"

"No. Because I'm an idiot. And because I lack an ounce of creativity in my own life, but it seems I'm better with yours. Here's an opportunity to win Alex back being handed to you on a silver platter!"

"How is a food truck market going to win Alex back?" She was slightly irritated.

"Oh, Lyra," Silas said, slumping against the fridge dramatically. "That's not the part that will win him back."

"Then I don't get it."

"Singing your *song* to him will get him back."

Her body stood still while her mind raced at a thousand miles an hour. For just a second, knowing it would break her heart later, she built a castle in the sky. She pictured a glorious reunion: her on stage and Alex in the crowd, staring at her the way he had that night at Rusty's. Her stepping off stage and into his arms, into his life again. The thought made her heart swell and the core of her body ache.

"Earth to Lyra," Silas joked, and reality came crashing back in. Alex wouldn't come, not even if she asked him. He hadn't returned text messages, why would he show up in person to hear a song from a woman he no longer cared about and had probably forgotten? And even if he heard her song, how could that make up for the way she'd embarrassed him and Steve, or what he thought had happened between her and Miles? For the lies she'd told, even without meaning to.

She shook her head sadly. "It won't work."

Silas rolled his eyes. "Listen to me. If you do this, I will try whatever you suggest with Ernie. Anything. I'll make an enormous fool of myself in the dumbest way you can dream up. But you have to try. Talk to Jenny when she's here tomorrow. Ask her to invite Alex. Tell her to lie if she has to."

"Yes, lies are a fabulous idea and they turn out so well for me."

Silas clicked his tongue. "You've *got* to try this, Lyra. It's breaking my heart to see you so sad, and I know he likes you too. I saw it the moment he first set eyes on you."

"He *did*," she said flatly. "But he doesn't anymore."

Silas shook his head. "It doesn't just evaporate."

She studied her brother's face as she considered what he was proposing. She rarely saw Silas so earnest. His big puppy-dog eyes were entreating her, something she'd never been able to refuse.

Finally she shrugged. "It's not going to work, but okay. I'll try. I have nothing else to lose with him."

Silas ran into the truck and hugged her. "Honestly, once he hears the lyrics to your song, he's probably going to propose on the spot."

She couldn't help but laugh. "Can we try dating and then living together for a while at least?" She smiled, but inside she felt hollow. Those words felt like a dream from another lifetime now - so very, very far from reach.

❖

The next day, all her resolve vanished into thin air. She'd dreamt about her date with Alex on the picnic blanket by the airfield. It had been so vivid that she'd woken bathed in sweat, her pulse galloping and her body throbbing. It seemed like a particularly unfair dream for her brain to create, and unnecessary. She didn't need help remembering how good it had felt to be with Alex; she needed Alex.

Silas was still pushing her to talk to Jenny, but her feet were glued to the floor.

"Go on," Silas said, practically shoving her out of the truck.

"It's pointless." She shook her head.

Silas heaved a sigh. "It might be," he agreed. "But I can tell you it's *guaranteed* that nothing will happen if you don't try. Go talk to her. She's just a human."

"A human cousin of Alex's who probably hates me."

"I will fire you if you don't go."

They glared at one another until it turned into giggles. "Okay, *fine*. But you have to let me walk to the Secret Garden when this all blows up in my face."

Jenny's face was expressionless as Lyra approached her. "Hi," Lyra said uneasily.

Jenny smiled, but the radiance Lyra had known before everything went bad with Alex was absent. "Hello," she replied flatly.

Lyra stood silent for a moment, until Jenny arched an eyebrow at her. "I...I wanted to ask you a favour," she mumbled. Jenny didn't respond, but indicated that she was listening. Lyra shoved the flyer at her. "I'd love you to somehow get Alex to come to this event. If - if you would."

Jenny took the flyer and studied it for a moment. "Why?" Her face was inscrutable.

Lyra took a deep breath and then rushed the words out as quickly as she could. "I made a huge mistake with Alex. I made a fool of us both at a meeting he got for me. I still can't even believe he managed to get me the meeting in the first place. And then on the same day, he... he thinks he saw something that he didn't."

Jenny frowned. "What does that mean?" she asked coolly.

"He thinks he saw me coming out of someone's flat. Another man's." She swallowed hard and squeezed her eyes shut for a moment, before forcing herself to continue. "And I was, but...not for the reason he thinks. That guy had told me he had a gig for me, and that we needed to talk about it. I thought it might at least be a way to make things up to Mick, my band member. But when I got there...it wasn't what it seemed at all. So I left."

Jenny's face had softened a little at the story. "He tried...?" She trailed off.

Lyra nodded. "He didn't force himself on me," she said quickly, in case a mixed-up story reached Alex's ears. "But he made it plain that if I wanted the gig, he'd need something in return."

Jenny nodded slowly. She seemed to be weighing something up. "Gross." She almost spat the word out. "Men like that should be castrated."

Lyra nodded in agreement. But she didn't care about Miles right now. She only needed to know if Jenny would help her with Alex.

Jenny looked at her intently. "You look tired."

Lyra looked down at the ground, tears threatening to well again. "I haven't really slept that well the last two months."

"And you've lost weight."

"I often haven't felt like eating…" Lyra tried to sound less pathetic than that sentence made her feel.

Jenny seemed to reach a decision. "I'll help." Her smile

showed real warmth for the first time. She looked at the flyer again. "Are you already registered as a musician?"

Lyra shook her head. "I didn't see any point unless he was going to be here. I kind of wrote a song. For him."

That was it for Jenny. She disappeared and came almost racing around from the back of the truck and wrapped Lyra in her warm hug. Lyra struggled to keep the tears back.

"He'll be here," Jenny said, smiling as she released Lyra. "I'll make absolutely certain of it."

CHAPTER THIRTY-SEVEN

The day of the festival, Lilac Bay looked stunning. The early evening light cast a mellow glow over the six or so food trucks that circled a small stage between the Secret Garden and the shoreline. The weather was perfect, the air warm and scented with lilac as the sun started to set on a perfect Sydney spring day.

Fairy lights had been strung up along the shoreline and a drinks truck was doing a roaring trade in the centre of it all. Small groups of people chatted or sat together on benches among the lilac bushes. Some had even brought their own folding chairs. An easy Friday-afternoon vibe permeated the scene. It was close to perfection.

Lyra, Marley and Amy were standing together behind The Pie-ganic. Lyra couldn't have imagined doing this without them in her corner, cheering her on.

"Is the song any good?" Marley asked, in her tactless way. "I mean, if you're going to all this trouble, it would be really embarrassing if it wasn't awesome."

Amy glared at Marley. "I can't kick you because of this dress, but I swear I would." She gestured to her mauve tweed pencil-dress which was showing off her curves to perfection. Lyra had seen more than a few men - and women - double-take in appreciation as Amy walked past.

"Okay," Marley said, holding up her hands and laughing a little, "I heard it after I said it." She turned to Lyra. "I'm sure it's amazing, and that he'll be running back into your arms."

Lyra knew from Marley's tone that she didn't get it. All this fuss over one guy? Lyra could almost feel Marley's shoulders fighting to suppress a shrug. Lyra didn't think Marley had felt the kind of connection she did with Alex. But Amy had. And Lyra sensed that Amy's excitement for her was tinged with sadness over Rick. They still weren't speaking, but Lyra also knew Rick hadn't given up. He wasn't making a nuisance of himself, just letting her know now and again, in his gentle way, that it was still her he wanted.

"It's the best thing I've ever written," Lyra said, firmly and confidently. *But will it be enough?* She tried to silence the doubts in her mind.

Amy wrapped her in a quick, fierce hug.

"We're going to go blend into the crowd and cheer like maniacs, okay?"

Lyra could hardly imagine them "blending in", Amy with her perfectly-styled retro vibe, standing beside tall Marley who was dressed in a WWII-era blazer paired with a pink tulle skirt. She'd teamed the outfit with a giant pair of brown "clod-hopper" boots, as Silas would call them, and she'd freshly cut her fringe into a delightfully lop-sided layer rather high above her eyebrows. Still, somehow tonight she looked like an haute-couture runway model with her bright eyes and incredible bone structure. Coco Chanel could have done a lot with her, Lyra decided.

The girls gave her one last quick hug each and disappeared, leaving her anxiously behind the truck. She stepped out to assess the situation and see whether she could spot

Alex. She couldn't, but she reminded herself there was still time.

Glancing at her watch, she realised Mick was late. Just as she had the thought, she saw him hurrying over to her - with Kathryn on his arm.

"Kiddo," he said. "We got a flat on the way."

"Of course you did," Lyra laughed, hugging him with nervous energy and smiling at Kathryn, who could barely keep her eyes off Mick. Lyra noticed that once she had released Mick from the hug, he subconsciously gravitated back to Kathryn and their hands found one another and clutched tight, even as they looked in Lyra's direction. Lyra swallowed hard, pushing away thoughts of her mother. Her hand flew to the locket and she mentally kissed her and asked for her help.

"Okay." Lyra drew a deep breath. "Are you ready?"

"Let's blow up that stage," Mick said, grinning.

There was chatter and the noise of glasses clinking, but the world was silent for Lyra as she took her place on the stage and scanned the crowd for Alex. She still couldn't see him anywhere. Her shoulders slumped.

People began to turn to her expectantly and she realised she was going to have to get on with the show, Alex or not. She spotted Amy and Marley in the crowd and gave them a small wave. They whooped and waved back crazily, making her smile. Another hand went up, close to the girls. It was Frank, who blew Lyra a kiss. She pretended to catch it and pull it to her chest. It was just the levity she needed, and a reminder of what she was there for. She was there to sing. She would have to put off dealing with her heartbreak until after that was done.

Lyra turned to Mick, who gave her a double thumbs up. She drew a deep breath. This was it. Showtime.

"Hi everyone," she said into the mic and instantly the crowd hushed a little. "My name is Lyra, this is my band mate Mick, and we'd like to sing a couple of songs for you tonight. Thanks for having us!"

There was a smattering of applause and they kicked off their set with an old original, one that was usually a crowd favourite. Tonight was no different. People swayed along to the song, chatted to one another quietly or grinned up at her, enjoying the music. A ripple of joy ran along her spine, making goosebumps break out on her arms as she looked at the happy faces among the crowd. It felt as though there was magic in the warm night air.

There was a burst of applause when she finished singing and she turned to Mick, who was grinning.

"Beatles?"

He nodded. "You choose," he said and she turned back to the crowd.

"Okay, now we're going to do a song you might have heard once or twice." She grinned. "This is one of my favourites. *I Saw Her Standing There.*"

The crowd cheered as they launched into the song. It was one they had played a thousand times together and it still brought them joy each time. Below Lyra, a middle-aged couple stood up and started dancing close to the stage. Several other couples quickly followed suit.

Lyra felt a smile spreading across her face despite the hole being eaten through her heart. Alex hadn't come. They weren't going to get back together and she had to find a way to be okay with that. She was reminded of how many beautiful moments life was full of. And that it was never certain how many of them a person would get to enjoy. All she could do was enjoy *this* beautiful moment, as much as she'd wished for a different ending.

She knew she'd go to pieces later. She had let herself believe he would be there, after Jenny's promise. And now she'd have to bury that hope entirely.

The applause was louder when they finished the song and it fed Lyra and Mick's energy. Mick was beaming, mopping a little perspiration off his forehead after having thrown himself into the song. She raised an eyebrow at him and he nodded. That was what Lyra loved about their dynamic. Entirely without words, they'd just agreed to keep doing covers, since the crowd was enjoying them so much.

They played *Girls Just Wanna Have Fun* next, as more couples and groups started dancing. The rest of the set was a blend of Beatles' songs, recent music and some older crowd favourites. For their second to last song, they decided on *(Your Love Keeps Lifting Me) Higher and Higher* and it seemed as though the entire crowd was either singing, dancing, smiling or swaying.

As Lyra's gaze moved over the crowd again, her heart snagged. He was there. She would have noticed him anywhere. His tall, well-built frame, close-cropped hair, his almost-uniform of jeans and a t-shirt...his grey-gold eyes. He was standing in front of Meat is Murder. Jenny was inside the truck, beaming out at Lyra. But he was there. Alex was there.

As the song came to a close, Lyra turned to Mick and gave him the signal. She was going to sing her new song. He put his hand on his chest and nodded, his eyes sparkling. Lyra turned back to the crowd, her heart pounding, and locked eyes with Alex. She couldn't read anything in his expression, but she didn't care. He was there, and she was going to sing for him. No matter what happened next, that would be enough.

"This is our last song for you tonight," she said to the crowd. "It's a little different from the last ones. It's written for someone I made a big mistake with. Someone who's...really, really special to me. Alex," she took a deep breath. "Alex, I started writing this song about you the first day I met you. I finally finished it and it's called *The Right Notes.*"

The crowd cheered and Lyra felt like she knew every single one of them. She felt as though she was surrounded by old friends. It was an incredible feeling. She didn't dare look at Alex again.

She took one deep, bracing inhale and then Mick started up the music. They hadn't had much time to rehearse the song, but as soon as they started, Lyra felt the familiar tingle of goosebumps that told her everything would work out perfectly. She closed her eyes and started singing. Instantly, a hush fell over the crowd and she knew she had everyone's attention. She let the music wash over her and sang with more of her heart and soul than she had ever sung before. The notes and melody pushed her voice to their limit and made the most of her range in a way she knew was a little haunting.

When she opened her eyes to launch into the chorus she saw Silas swaying and mouthing along with the words, his hand on his heart. She saw her girls with huge grins plastered on their faces, and watched as an involuntary shiver ran through Marley, who nodded at Lyra.

Finally, she looked at Alex. He was looking right back at her, drinking in every word. It was as though they were the only two people there. Just like the first moment he had ever heard her sing, that strange Tuesday not a hundred metres from this spot.

But this time, every word was written just for him and her voice hit every note perfectly. His eyes were locked on hers, a slow smile spreading over his face. He quickly whispered something to Jenny and Cameron, who both grinned and slapped his shoulder. Then he started weaving his way through the crowd towards her.

The closer he got, the bigger Lyra's smile became, until soon he was standing right before her and she was singing him his song. Straight into his beautiful eyes and that sensuous mouth that was curved into a transfixed half-smile. All she wanted was for the song to finish so she could jump off the stage and into his arms.

She sang the last notes of the song with a grin so wide she thought her face would split in two. As soon as she was finished, Alex closed the gap to the stage and held his arms out. To the thunderous applause of everyone present, Lyra jumped into his arms and he spun her around.

She buried her head into his neck and breathed in the scent of him, feeling a tingle ripple all the way through her body. She kissed his neck, his jaw, his cheek. And then their lips met and they melted into one another, all of the passion, pain and hope they'd felt during their separation making the kiss hot, urgent and lingering.

"I'm so sorry, Alex," she said, when they finally broke apart, both breathless and pink-cheeked. He hugged her tight, the safe haven of his arms reassuring her that she was forgiven.

"No, I'm sorry," he murmured into her ear. "I've been an idiot, and I should never have let you go."

A cheer went up from the crowd as Lyra heard Mick launch into a spontaneous solo keyboard rendition of *She Loves You* by the Beatles.

Suddenly, Alex and Lyra were rushed upon by Jenny. "Did you tell her?" Jenny demanded, a huge grin on her face.

"Tell me what?" Lyra said, not wanting to remove her arms from around Alex's waist. Alex looked coy.

"He organised this whole thing!" Jenny was gleeful,

sweeping her arm around to indicate the whole bay. Lyra pulled back and looked at Alex, who was grinning.

"What?"

"He set all this up, organised the permits, hired the other bands, called in the food trucks and even did the décor!" Jenny continued proudly.

Lyra slapped Alex playfully and then melted into his arms again. "I thought I had seen you around here a few times! Why?" she asked, tilting her face up to him.

"For you, silly." His voice was husky. "I wanted you to get a second chance."

"With you?" she asked hopefully.

"You don't need a second chance with me, you're stuck with me I'm afraid." He pulled her closer into a hug that promised much more once they were alone. Lyra's pulse raced. "I tried so hard to forget you, but it was pointless. It's been you, ever since the first day I saw you." He traced a finger down her cheek, a tender look in his eyes. "I wanted a second chance for you with Selena."

At that moment, Selena Teller joined the group and Lyra put a hand over her mouth.

"I am so, so, sorry, Selena-" she started to say, but Selena flapped her hand dismissively.

"You don't have to say a thing after that performance," she said. "Steve and Alex were right, you're a real talent. Let's organise another meeting next week."

Lyra could barely believe her ears and she looked from face to smiling face, burying her head temporarily against Alex's firm chest to hide her bursting grin.

"No Margot this time." Selena winked when Lyra looked up again. She laughed and nodded in agreement.

"Come on," Jenny said to Selena. "Let's go grab a drink."

They disappeared, leaving Lyra alone with Alex. And as

Mick continued on stage and everyone around them danced, she and Alex locked eyes.

Her face was glowing and the joy she felt was reflected in his eyes. Slowly, so slowly, he leaned in and kissed her. She kissed him back, hard, wrapping her arms tightly around him. She knew she'd never let him go again.

THE END

SECOND CHANCES AT LILAC BAY

(LILAC BAY BOOK 2)

When you have everything, you have everything to lose...

Amy Porter has it all; a high-flying career, supportive friends, and the world's most devoted boyfriend.

But when a startling revelation rocks her relationship with Rick to the core, she feels she has no choice but to walk away from the love of her life.

As though things aren't bad enough, Amy's career hits a rocky patch and her friendships fray under pressure.

It takes a tragedy for her to realise she doesn't need a picture-perfect life. What she needs is to be surrounded by people she loves.

Now she must fight for all she holds dear.

Can she win back her soul mate and rebuild her friendships? Will she find the courage to take a leap of faith with her career?

One thing's for certain: Amy will do whatever it takes for a second chance at happiness.

Set on the breathtaking coastline of Bondi Beach and Sydney Harbour, Second Chances at Lilac Bay is a sweet romance about love, hope and healing.

ACKNOWLEDGMENTS

Giving birth to my literal child was easier than finishing this - my first - book, although considerably less fun (the child himself is beyond delightful. Labour was not).

First, my thanks go to Anthea Kirk, for giving me the encouragement I needed to get started. Thank you for your cherished friendship, insightful input and feedback, and for giving me that first push.

To my wonderful sister, Catherine Maloney, who scans everything I write with a teacher's eye, a reader's mind and a sister's heart. I love you, sissy!

To the amazing Hannah, for motivation, invaluable advice, feedback, input and encouragement. And mostly, for friendship. I wouldn't be trying this without a role model like you.

To my editor Katharine D'Souza for knowing how to make it all even better, to the ladies at The Enchanted Quill for their services and support, and to my cover designer Ana Grigoriu-Voicu.

To my husband Kyle, who makes me happy every single day. I am eternally grateful for the string of coincidences that led to our meeting.

To Wyatt, my son, who seems destined for a career in IT with the way he can make a whole page disappear with the click of a button I've never before or after found on my laptop. I love you, Bug.

And to my Mama, who I hope can see this.

ABOUT THE AUTHOR

Marie Taylor-Ford is a wife, mother, knitter and devoted carboholic - not in that order.

Born in Wales and raised in Australia (Newy forever!), she's currently based in Munich, Germany where she's lived for over a decade.

If she's not writing, she's probably hanging out with her family or friends, traveling, knitting, reading, swearing at her FitOn app or gently coaxing her child into wearing the things she knitted for him.

You are warmly invited to stop by her website, www.marietaylorford.com, or connect via social media:

facebook.com/marietaylorford
instagram.com/marietaylorford

Printed in Great Britain
by Amazon